# Math and Manners

### Adventures in Reason

## Kris Langman

Post Hoc Publishing

# Chapter One

◆◆◆

## Fire in the Night

ALL NIKKI COULD see was a swirling cloud of white. Her first thought was a snowstorm, but as her mind cleared she remembered the flour. She struggled to her feet, rivulets of flour cascading down her hair. Her nose and mouth were choked with it. A coughing fit shook her. When she wiped her mouth with her hand a rivulet of blood spread across her palm. She gingerly felt along her jaw. Several of her teeth were loose. She leaned against the wall of the flour mill, grateful for the support of its thick stones, grateful to be alive. As her vision cleared she could see that the wall opposite her had collapsed. Only its huge supporting timbers were still standing.

She sneezed, sending a small puff of flour into the dusty air. There was something odd about the sneeze, but at first her hazy mind couldn't identify it. Then suddenly she realized that she hadn't heard the sneeze. She smacked her palm on the stone wall she was leaning against. Nothing. No sound at all. The explosion had made her temporarily deaf. It was very unnerving. If there was someone in the building with her she had no way of hearing them.

She cautiously peered over the edge of the staircase she was standing on. Its bannister had been destroyed in the blast and her head spun as she looked down. She quickly backed against the stone wall again, but the brief glimpse revealed that the floor below had been

1

destroyed in the blast. The moonlight shone on piles of burst flour sacks two stories below.

Ava. The Duchess of Falsa's maid. Where was she? Nikki looked frantically up and down the staircase. She and Ava had been running down the staircase when the explosion happened. Hugging the wall, she cautiously descended the staircase, feeling it sway at each step. The bolts attaching the stairs to the stone wall had come loose in places. Nikki increased her pace. She didn't want to be on the stairs if they came crashing down. She had almost reached the destroyed floor below her when she came to a halt. The rest of the staircase was gone, blown apart by the blast. She was just about to turn around and climb back up when she saw the body, two floors below. It was Ava. Her dark blue dress was covered in flour and a pool of blood surrounded her head. Nikki sank to her knees, tears pouring down her face. Even from this distance she knew Ava was dead, either from the explosion or from the impact with the stone floor of the flour mill. It was sheer luck that Nikki herself hadn't met the same fate.

Nikki sat there for a long while, unable to look away from the body, unable to hear her own sobs. Finally, painfully, she got to her feet. She couldn't do anything to bring Ava back to life, but she had a responsibility to tell someone of her death. She could tell Ava's sister. She tried to remember everything Ava had told her during their brief conversation in the Duchess of Falsa's front parlor. Ava's sister worked as a maid for Lady Hyacinth, a powerful noblewoman who lived in a part of Cogent Town called Clearwater Gardens. Lady Hyacinth was sympathetic to the imps and Nikki and Ava had been headed to her mansion to try to enlist her help. Ava had said that Lady Hyacinth's mansion was somewhere along the Clearwater River, and had been leading Nikki toward the river before they'd turned aside to investigate the fireworks being shot from the flour mill.

Movement caught her eye. She watched as a heavy wooden beam attached to the opposite wall broke loose and fell to the stone floor far below. The crash sent up a huge plume of flour but she still heard nothing. She had to get out of the building before it came crashing down on her head. Since she couldn't go down the only way out was up. She retraced her steps up the shaky staircase. When she reached the top floor landing she paused. Geber and the man from the Mystic Mountains had been launching the fireworks from this floor. She wasn't sure which she dreaded more, finding them alive or finding them dead. She clenched her fists and forced herself to enter the room at the top of the building. She wasn't surprised to find a huge hole torn through the oak beams of the floor. The wall facing the street was gone and the room was cold from the night air. Splinters from destroyed flour barrels were everywhere, scattered across what remained of the floor.

Nikki inched across the floor, keeping her back to the remaining wall. When she reached the opening onto the street she looked down. The cobblestone street was dusted with flour like a blanket of snow. The street was empty and she wondered why no one was running toward the explosion. Then she remembered that all the imps in this part of Cogent Town had been rushing to put out the fires caused by Geber's fireworks. She could see a few of the fireworks littering the street, little cylinders with a short fuse at one end. One of them was lying next to a pile of rags in front of the flour mill. Suddenly Nikki turned away, trying not to be sick. The body was badly smashed, but she recognized part of the robe which covered it. There was an alchemist symbol on one of the sleeves. It was Geber.

She leaned against the wall, her stomach churning. Was she the only survivor of the explosion? The body of the Mystic man wasn't down on the cobblestones. She peered around the moonlit room. The explosion had destroyed the flour barrels which had been stacked in neat pyramids. The room now seemed empty except for what looked like a kind of chute protruding from one wall. Nikki guessed that it was used to slide sacks of flour down to the street. She carefully edged over to it, wondering if she could use it to get out of the building. She could just make out a pile of what looked like flour sacks lumped in a dark corner under the chute.

As she drew nearer the hair on the back of her neck stood up. It wasn't a pile of sacks but another body. It was the Mystic man. He was lying on his side up against the wall where the explosion had thrown him. His legs were twisted under him at unnatural angles, but otherwise he was less crushed than Geber. She could make out the empty socket of his missing eye which had pulsed so unpleasantly in life. She didn't feel any sadness at his death. He'd been a cruel, violent man. As she stood looking at him, a thought started to form. He had such a strong hold over his followers. They followed him blindly, as if he were some kind of cult leader. Nikki felt sure that the Mystic men would still be holed up in their hideout in the Mystic Mountains if their leader hadn't ordered them to follow him to Cogent Town. If they found out he was dead they'd be leaderless. It would cause confusion in their ranks and uncertainty about what to do. They might even give up their plan to set fire to Cogent Town. They might leave and go back to their hideout. It would be a huge blow to Rufius and his quest for power if he could no longer count on the Mystic men to do his dirty work for him.

A sprinkle of flour fell on her head and she glanced up. A large crack had formed in the ceiling and it was getting wider. If she left the body of the Mystic man here there was a good chance it would be crushed when the ceiling caved in. The body might become unrecognizable and his followers would never learn what had happened to him. They might hang around Cogent Town, waiting for him to come back.

She glanced from the body to the chute. Better to do it at once, before she had time to think about it. She grabbed the body under the shoulders and dragged it to the opening. The chute was low to the floor and she was able to load the body in like a twisted sack of flour.

When she let go the body quickly disappeared from sight. A little too quickly, Nikki thought worriedly, peering down the chute. In the darkness she couldn't tell how steep the chute was. Maybe she should find another way down. She was about to head back to the staircase when the ceiling of the room suddenly came crashing down. The timbers of the ceiling crashed through the hole in the floor and a huge cloud of flour dust swirled through the room.

Nikki wasted no time. She climbed into the chute, bracing her feet against the metal sides. She put out her hands to try to slow her descent, but as soon as she pulled her feet off the sides of the chute she took off at a terrifying speed. She pulled her hands in and closed her eyes tightly. The first few seconds of her slide were blindingly fast, but then the pace began to slow. Nikki felt an odd softness on her arms and her nose became clogged. Flour. The bottom of the chute was filled with flour. She fought with panic as her pace slowed even more. If the flour got any deeper she would suffocate. She was now barely moving. Keeping her eyes and mouth tightly shut she tried to swim through the flour with her arms, pushing it against the sides of the chute. Her pace increased a little and she attacked the flour with her legs also, moving them back and forth as if creating a snow angel. It seemed to take an eternity, but foot by foot she swam down the clogged chute. Just when she felt she couldn't hold her breath for another second she felt her feet hit something. It had to be the body of the Mystic man, blocking the chute. Nikki kicked frantically at it and felt it slowly slide down the chute. A few more seconds and she was abruptly dumped onto the hard cobblestones of the street.

She scrambled to her feet and shook herself like a wet dog, sending a cloud of flour out into the cold night air. She wiped the flour out of her eyes and blew it out of her nose. When she was able to see again the first thing she noticed was the Mystic man. He had landed on his back in the street. He was coated in flour, but his face with its distinctive empty eye-socket was clearly visible. She looked up at the damaged flour mill. Her heart crumpled, knowing that she would have to leave Ava's body inside. It was too dangerous to go back in. She could feel the stones under her feet vibrating as the walls of the mill swayed back and forth. She walked quickly away from the mill, glancing at the buildings nearby. Fortunately this street was lined with warehouses. She didn't see any houses where people might be living. If the mill did collapse it was unlikely to hurt anyone else.

She paused at the first intersection she came to, trying to get her bearings. She could hear the crackle of fire behind her, the first sound she'd heard since the explosion. It was a relief to know that her hearing was returning. She could smell the smoke from the buildings Geber had set alight with his fireworks. To her right she could just make out the tip of Castle Cogent's tallest tower shining in the moonlight. Ava had been leading her away from the castle toward the north end of town, heading for the Clearwater River. Nikki made her best guess as to the direction of the river and took off at a fast walk along a street which seemed headed that way.

After several miles of hard walking the half-timbered houses, pubs, and shops in the center of Cogent Town began to give way to large houses with hedges surrounding them. Marble-covered mansions began to appear, set far back from the road. Nikki hoped that she had managed to find Clearwater Gardens. She could hear the river rushing nearby. She scrambled down a steep bank covered in rhododendron bushes and emerged on narrow strip of sandy beach carved by the river. The Clearwater River was narrow and fast-moving, its waters white with boulder-filled rapids. An owl was hooting nearby but otherwise the riverbank was deserted. She headed upriver along the beach, passing turreted mansions with rose gardens overlooking the river. It was past midnight and most of the mansions were dark, but a few had candles still shining in the windows. She wondered how she was going to figure out which mansion was Lady Hyacinth's. She didn't want to risk asking someone. She was still wearing her page uniform, but it was covered in flour. Plus she'd lost her page hat in the explosion at the flour mill. The hat was a big part of her disguise. Without it she was much more likely to be recognized.

She rounded a sharp bend in the river and came to a halt. Ahead of her stretched a huge expanse of well-manicured lawn bordering the river. A stone jetty extended from the edge of the lawn into the river. At the far side of the lawn rose an immense mansion, its roof garnished with an astonishing number of towers, turrets, and gables. It looked nearly as big as Castle Cogent. Candelabras shone in its many windows and torches bolted to its marble walls blazed with light. Nikki could see the outlines of people as they passed in front of the windows, and there were dozens of carriages parked on the mansion's gravel drive. It looked like some sort of party was going on.

Nikki stood frowning at the mansion. Judging by the size of the building this was very possibly the home of Lady Hyacinth, but she couldn't be sure. She didn't want to risk talking with people unless she absolutely had to. She looked down at her flour-covered uniform. She needed another disguise. A servant's costume would be the best. Upper-class party goers wouldn't look closely at a servant.

Nikki scrambled up the sandy riverbank and stepped hesitantly onto the smooth lawn. An awful thought suddenly popped into her head. What if there were guard dogs? There were no trees to climb anywhere on the flat expanse of grass. She stood listening as hard as she could, but all she could hear was the rushing of the river and a faint tinkle of laughter from the party. Taking a deep breath she broke into a sprint. It there were dogs maybe she could reach the building before they caught her scent.

The lawn seemed endless and her heart was pounding in her ears, but she finally made it across unmolested by either guards or guard dogs. She threw herself into the dark shadow cast by a chimney and leaned against its bricks to catch her breath. She could hear the clink of glasses and the voices of many people but she couldn't make out what they were saying. She'd deliberately headed for a dark corner of the building, away from the lighted windows. Now all she needed was a way in. She was wondering if she could climb the thick strands of ivy wrapped around the chimney when suddenly one of the bricks she was leaning against moved. Startled, she poked cautiously at it. The mortar holding the brick in place crumbled, and with a plop it suddenly fell inward into the chimney.

Nikki ran her hands across the bricks nearby. Many of them wobbled at the slightest touch. She pushed and pulled at them. Some fell onto the grass and others fell inward. Soon she had a hole in the side of the chimney big enough to crawl through. She put an arm into the hole and waved it around, feeling nothing but empty space. Whoever maintained the building ought to be fired, Nikki thought as she crawled through the hole.

Once inside she held back a sneeze as the smell of soot filled her nose. She was crouching in a pile of it, but it was cold and damp. A fire hadn't been lit inside the chimney for a long time. A tall metal grate blocked the chimney from the rest of the room. Nikki peered through its bars. Moonlight shone through dusty windows and she could make out ghostly white shapes scattered across the floor. They were large and lumpy and Nikki soon realized that they were pieces of furniture covered in white sheets. The room was clearly not being used. She carefully pulled one edge of the grate open and crawled out of the fireplace.

She left footprints as she walked across the dusty floor but decided it wasn't worth the effort to wipe them out. This was the Realm, not modern-day Wisconsin. The Rounders of Cogent Town weren't capable of tracking her based just on footprints. If anyone came into the room and noticed the footprints they'd probably just assume a servant had made them. She lifted an edge of the sheet covering a rectangular piece of furniture. Just a table. She let the sheet drop and tried a taller object up against one wall. This was more promising. It was a chest of drawers. She pulled open the top drawer and found it filled to the brim with fans. The type used by aristocratic ladies in eighteenth century France to flirt with courtiers. They were beautifully painted, but definitely not the sort of thing a servant would use. The other drawers were also unhelpful. They were packed with silk and satin dresses, lace shawls, and elaborate hats with veils. Nikki shut the drawers and pulled the white sheet back over the chest.

As quickly as she could she tried all the other furniture in the room. There were a few other chests in the room but none held clothing. Reluctantly, Nikki returned to the chest of drawers and opened the drawer filled with silk dresses. She stared down at them with a sinking feeling in her stomach. Dressing as a servant had seemed like a safe idea. She could skirt the edges of any room in the mansion and go unnoticed. But dressing as a noblewoman in a silk dress meant that people might try to talk to her. And there was also the problem of her age and her accent. It seemed unlikely that any fourteen-year-olds had been invited to a fancy party that was still going strong after midnight. She opened the drawer with all the hats and rummaged through them. A piece of black lace caught her eye and she pulled on it. It was attached to a small red silk hat. The black lace hung down from it like a veil and was big enough to cover her face down to the chin. Nikki sighed. This costume was going to require acting, and acting was not among her talents.

Before she could talk herself out of it she quickly pulled off her flour-covered page uniform and stuffed it into the drawer filled with dresses. She pulled a red silk gown on over her Westlake Debate Team T-shirt. The gown had a high neck and elbow-length sleeves which hid the T-shirt. The gown was a little bit baggy on her, but not enough that anyone would notice. She wound her long dark hair into a ponytail and shoved it under the silk hat, pulling the black lace down over her face. Leaning forward to check the skirt of the gown for any flour-smudges she noticed that her scuffed page shoes were peeking out. She rummaged through all the drawers again and found a pair of red silk slippers under the painted fans. They were too big for her, but after stuffing silk handkerchiefs in the toes she was able to walk in them. She closed all the drawers and carefully pulled the sheet back down over the chest.

Okay, Nikki thought. Time to be somebody else. She would keep her voice low to make herself sound older, but she also needed something to explain her accent. For some reason Bertie's story about his travels outside the Realm popped into her head. She would pretend to be from Friebergen, the little town north of the Realm that Bertie had talked about. He had made it sound like not many people from the Realm traveled there. Hopefully there weren't any Friebergers at the party tonight.

# Chapter Two

## High Society

NIKKI STOOD INDECISIVELY in the doorway to the ballroom. It hadn't been hard to find. She'd just followed the sound of music and loud laughter. Dozens of guests were whirling around the room in a fast-paced waltz, the ladies' dresses floating like silk flowers. Small tables were placed against the mirrored walls where people sipped champagne as they watched the dancers. A few were playing cards.

"Excuse me, Miss. Coming through."

Nikki spun around. A young servant girl was trying to maneuver a fancy wheeled cart through the doorway. A silver teapot and plates of pastries were piled on the cart.

"Ava," gasped Nikki. The resemblance was astonishing. The girl could almost be Ava's identical twin.

"Did you say something, Miss?" asked the girl. "It almost sounded like you said 'Ava'. But most likely I'm just imagining things. I have a sister called Ava, you see, and I was just thinking about her. She works as a lady's maid for the Duchess of Falsa, in one of those big houses near the castle. I usually work as a lady's maid too, but tonight we're so short of staff that I got recruited to deliver the pastries. Lady Hyacinth's parties always have lots of guests, but this one's a real whopper. Seems like every noble in Cogent Town is here."

The girl wrangled her cart through the doorway, leaving Nikki staring after her.

Ava's sister. Nikki couldn't decide if it was good luck or bad. Now she knew that she had found Lady Hyacinth's mansion, but the awful task of having to tell this girl about Ava's death suddenly loomed in front of her. She was about to go find a quiet corner away from the ballroom where she could wait for Ava's sister when she suddenly felt an arm wrap around her waist. She was propelled into the midst of the swirling dancers.

"Your left arm goes up on my shoulder, my dear."

"Oh, right," said Nikki, snatching a quick glance up at the tall man who was spinning her around the ballroom at a dizzying pace. He was an older man of about seventy, with white hair, a white goatee and startling blue eyes. His blue satin frock coat matched his eyes.

"Allow me to introduce myself," said the man as he expertly steered Nikki away from another couple who was about to collide with them. "I am the Count of Calumnia. Lady Hyacinth spotted you standing in the doorway and asked me to intervene. You looked a bit lost."

"Oh," said Nikki. "Yes. I suppose I was. I just turned eighteen, you see, and this is my first really big party. I find it quite intimidating."

"You are here with your parents, I presume?" asked the Count.

"No, it's just me," said Nikki. "My parents are back home in Freibergen. They sent me to Cogent Town so I could see some of the Realm. I've never travelled outside of my home town before. I'm staying with my cousin."

"I see," said the Count, sounding polite but bored.

Nikki glanced up at him and noticed that he was staring at a group of people playing cards at one of the side tables. She felt herself being steered in that direction, the Count expertly weaving in and out of the other dancers until they arrived at the table.

"Here you are, my dear," said the Count, depositing her on a gilded chair against the wall, not far from the card players. "I hope you enjoyed our dance." He made her an elegant little bow and took his place at the card table.

One of the ladies playing cards turned in her seat and tapped Nikki lightly on the knee with her fan. "I hope the Count didn't startle you too much, my dear. It was my idea that he ask you to dance. Though I noticed that he didn't so much ask as grab. He sometimes has to be reminded of his manners. Counts are just below the King on the social ladder and it tends to go to their heads. But don't worry, this one is harmless."

"So you're Lady Hyacinth," Nikki blurted out.

The lady's eyebrows arched in surprise.

Nikki blushed under her veil. "I'm sorry. It's just that I've never met you before. I'm new in town and I'm staying with my cousin. She let me have her invitation to this party. She said that you were an elderly lady who walks with a cane, but I see that she was completely mistaken. You can't be more than forty."

Lady Hyacinth smiled at her and tapped her with the fan again, this time a little harder. "Don't try flattery on me, young lady. I don't respond to it and you have no talent for it." She patted her grey hair. It matched her grey silk gown and was twisted into a sedate bun at the back of her neck. "I just turned seventy and I look it. And I do walk with a cane when my arthritis flares up, not that it is any of your business." She stared intently at Nikki as if trying to see through her veil. "You have an unusual accent, my dear. I can't quite place it."

"I'm from Freibergen," said Nikki. "This is my first visit to the Realm."

Lady Hyacinth's eyebrows arched even higher in her lightly powdered face. "Really? How odd. You don't sound at all like a Freiberger. One of my oldest friends lives there and I've visited her many times over the years. Her accent is much more guttural than yours. She sounds like she has a frog drowning in her throat. I'm always teasing her about it."

Nikki stared back at her, not knowing what to say. Lady Hyacinth sat patiently watching her, as if determined to wait for an explanation. Finally in desperation Nikki decided it was time to drop the act. It wasn't working anyway, and Athena had said that Lady Hyacinth was a friend to the imps. "Have you seen Fuzz or Athena lately?" she asked.

Whatever explanation her host had been expecting it wasn't this. Lady Hyacinth dropped her fan and stared at Nikki, her eyes wide.

The Count of Calumnia put his cards face down on the table and retrieved the fan, handing it to Lady Hyacinth with a little bow. "Madame, you look pale. Are you all right?"

Lady Hyacinth nodded distractedly. "Yes, I'm fine. Here, Count. Why don't you play my cards? I have quite a good hand. You can have my winnings too. I'm up to thirty gold coins. I need to talk to this young lady. She is the daughter of a good friend of mine and we have some catching up to do. Please excuse us." She gestured at Nikki to rise and walked arm in arm with her out of the ballroom.

"Where are we going?" asked Nikki, increasing her pace to keep up with Lady Hyacinth, who was walking surprisingly fast for a seventy-year-old with occasional arthritis.

"Up to my private chambers," replied Lady Hyacinth. "Now hurry, my dear. If we dawdle I'll be besieged with requests from every guest who wants something from me. And believe me, there are many of them. Usually they want money. There are many here like the Count of Calumnia who are addicted to card-playing. They lose everything and then expect me to bail them out just because their losses occurred at my house. I suppose I should stop holding card games at my parties, but I like a bit of card-playing myself. Though I have the sense to stop playing when I'm on a losing streak." She waved away a young woman who was crying into a handkerchief. The young woman snatched at Lady Hyacinth's arm but was brushed aside. "Ugh," said Lady Hyacinth. "The daughter of the Duke of Summerstone. She loses at every card game she plays. Her parents have very rightly cut her off. Now she turns on the waterworks and begs money from everyone she meets. If you give her any she heads straight for the card tables."

Nikki looked dubiously back at the crying young woman. She had collapsed onto a chair and was wailing so loudly that the chandelier above her head was vibrating. Lady Hyacinth's treatment of her seemed a bit harsh. Nikki had expected that someone who was a friend of the imps would be a bit nicer. She also thought that the Realm could use a few chapters of Gamblers Anonymous.

Lady Hyacinth chuckled as if reading Nikki's mind. "Stop judging me, my dear. I can tell you have no experience with gamblers. They'll steal you blind if you let them. Firmness, that's how you handle them." She led Nikki up a long flight of stairs covered with an elegant purple carpet. Its mahogany banisters were carved into the shape of herons, each with a wooden fish in its mouth. At the top of the stairs they continued down a long hallway, their feet sinking into the thick carpet. Portraits of people who Nikki assumed were Lady Hyacinth's ancestors lined the walls.

"In here, my dear," said Lady Hyacinth, steering Nikki through a broad oak doorway.

The bedroom they entered was even grander than the ones in Castle Cogent. It seemed to span half the length of the entire mansion. Huge windows stretched from floor to ceiling, overlooking the immense lawn which Nikki had run across. Past the lawn the rapids of the Clearwater River shone white under the moon light.

Lady Hyacinth shut and locked the bedroom door before lighting a candelabra which stood on a table near the windows. "Sit down, my dear," she said. "I'll just be a moment."

Nikki took a seat at the table and watched in surprise as Lady Hyacinth got down on her knees and peered under an enormous canopied bed covered in a blue silk bedspread.

"I hid it under here," said Lady Hyacinth, her voice muffled under the bedspread. "I've tried for years to train our maids to clean under the beds but they never do. This is the first time I've been grateful for their laziness." She re-emerged, holding a small book covered in leather. "No, it's not my diary," she said as she sat down next to Nikki at the table. "It's something much more important. Possibly. Maybe. Actually I'm not sure. The problem is that I can't read it."

Nikki's eyebrows arched in surprise.

"No, I don't mean that I can't read," said Lady Hyacinth, rolling her eyes. "Silly girl. Of course I can read. What I mean is that it's in code." She opened the little book to the first page and pushed it in front of Nikki.

Nikki pulled the candelabra closer and squinted at the book. It did appear to be in code. She couldn't read the odd symbols on the page any better than Lady Hyacinth could. She supposed it could be a foreign language, but she didn't think so. There was something familiar about the way words were spaced and how long they were. The symbols were written horizontally and grouped into paragraphs with the familiar blank line between each one. She flipped through the book. All of the pages were covered in the same symbols. There was nothing written on the leather cover. She looked up at Lady Hyacinth. "Why are you showing me this?" she asked. "You don't even know who I am."

Lady Hyacinth chuckled. "Of course I know who you are, my dear. You're the companion of Athena and Fuzz, the King's emissaries. You've been traveling the Realm with them for the better part of a year now."

Nikki's eyes widened in fear and she jumped up from her chair.

Lady Hyacinth grabbed her arm. "Sit down, my dear. I'm sorry. I didn't mean to frighten you. I've known Athena and Fuzz all their lives. They are dear friends of mine, and any friend of theirs is a friend of mine."

"But," stammered Nikki, sitting down again. "That doesn't explain how you know who I am."

Lady Hyacinth waved an impatient hand. "It was child's play, my dear. Your description has been on wanted posters all over the Realm for months now. A young woman under fifteen years of age seen traveling in the company of imps. A slight build and long dark hair. And an unusual accent. By the way, your hair is falling out from under your hat. Why don't you take off that silly hat and veil so I can see you better?"

Nikki reluctantly pulled off the hat and put it on the table. After spending so many days in disguise it felt strange to have someone looking directly at her face, without having it hidden under a veil or shadowed by a purple velvet page cap.

"No, you're definitely not a Freiberger," said Lady Hyacinth. "They tend to have red cheeks and pug noses. A cheerful people, but not very attractive. Anyway, now that we've got your identity straightened out, on to more important things." She tapped a finger on the little book. "This came to me in a very complicated manner which I won't bore you with. Suffice it to say that this little book may hold information vital to the safety of the Realm. It belonged to the Knights of the Iron Fist. One of their members deserted from their ranks and brought this book to a noble who lives here in Cogent Town. This book is not the original. It is a copy that the man made before leaving the Knights. So they are aware of his desertion but not aware that he took this book with him. The original is still in their hands."

"Why do you think this is important?" asked Nikki, leafing through the book again.

"Because the man said so," answered Lady Hyacinth. "He said the book described a plot between the Knights and Rufius, the little twit who has replaced old Maleficious as the King's adviser. An evil plot to destroy Cogent Town. Then, in the chaos after the destruction of the city, Rufius would take over as King of the Realm, with the Knights of the Iron Fist as his private army. Of course, the man who sold this book could be lying. Maybe it's just a book of recipes owned by a chef in D-ville who wrote it in code to hide the fact that his famous pumpernickel bread has bits of dried cow dung in it to give it flavor."

"Did the man get paid a lot for the book?" asked Nikki.

"Oh, yes," said Lady Hyacinth. "Many gold coins. So, yes, this could just be a con of his. Selling worthless books and making up stories about their origin to increase the price."

"Did his story include any more details?" asked Nikki. "How exactly do they plan to destroy Cogent Town?"

"I don't know," said Lady Hyacinth. "The man took his gold coins and disappeared. He wouldn't allow the buyer to see inside the book, so it was only after he left that the buyer realized that it was in code. I suspect the man couldn't read the code either. My guess is he just copied the symbols as carefully as he could from the original."

Nikki's thoughts went to the meeting in front of the fireplace in the library of the Prince of Physics. To the story of the Clearwater dam which Fortuna had told after being bribed with a bag of gold. The destruction of the dam would cause the type of chaos that Lady Hyacinth was describing. It seemed likely that this book held information about the same plot. If it had details about when and how the dam was to be destroyed that would immensely helpful. She looked down at the book doubtfully. She was fond of crossword puzzles, and one of her high school computer classes had briefly covered decryption, but she wasn't at all sure she could crack the book's code. Still, she had to try.

"Could you please get me a quill, ink, and some parchment?" she asked Lady Hyacinth.

Lady Hyacinth crossed the room to an ornate writing desk whose legs were covered in gold leaf. She returned with the items and placed them in front of Nikki.

Nikki scratched a long table of rows and columns onto the parchment and then entered each symbol on the first page of the book into each cell of the table. She then carefully counted the number of times each symbol appeared on the page and entered the total into its cell. A likely candidate appeared at once, but to be sure she flipped to the second page and entered those totals as well. "Yep," she said, pointing with the quill. "I'm pretty sure this funny little symbol that looks like a daisy is the letter E."

Lady Hyacinth blinked at her in bafflement. "Why do you think that, my dear? It could be any letter at all. Or the whole book could be just meaningless gibberish."

"The letter E is the most common letter in the alphabet," said Nikki. "In *our* alphabet, anyway." The question of why both she and Lady Hyacinth had the same alphabet immediately popped into her head. The issue of why she could understand the language spoken and written in the Realm had tortured her for many weeks after her arrival, but she'd forced herself to stop thinking about it. Her thoughts had gotten hopelessly tangled up in multiple universes, dreams, alternate realities, and portals between worlds. It had caused her many sleepless nights and even a few minor panic attacks. She could feel her anxiety rising right now. She forced herself to stop thinking about the whole mess. The Realm was in danger and many lives could be at risk. She'd have time for metaphysical wondering and multiple worlds later. Right now she was in *this* world and she had to deal with it.

"E is about twelve percent of the letters in any written text," she continued. "Ask any crossword puzzle addict. Now, we also know that the word 'the' is the most common word in the language. So, we just examine the text for any three-letter words ending in our daisy symbol." She bent over the book. "Yep, there are five of those on the first page alone. The first symbol in those three-letter groups looks kind of like an eye." She found the symbol on her parchment and put the letter T next to it. "And the middle symbol looks like a tiny tree. So that would be the letter H." She added it to her parchment. "There. We've now got the letters E, T, and H. Of course, I could be wrong, but let's keep going anyway. The next thing to look for is single letters by themselves. There are seven of these on the first page. The most likely candidates are the letters I and A. As in '*I* see *A* dog.' There's no way to tell yet which of these two symbols is I and which is A, but I'll make a note of that." She frowned down at the book. "After those obvious crossword-type clues it gets harder. The next step is to tackle some of the shorter words. Here's a five-symbol word which contains two of the T symbols. And one E symbol is in front of the two T's, and one is right after them also. There are several words I can think of right away which match that pattern: letter, wetter, and better. It could be any of them. They'd all be reasonable within the context of the subject matter."

"The subject matter being the plot to destroy Cogent Town?" asked Lady Hyacinth.

Nikki nodded. "At this point a lot of the decoding work is going to be trial-and-error. We have a good candidate for the letter R, as all three of our possible words end in that letter." She marked that symbol on the parchment. "And we have possible symbol candidates for the letters L, W, and B." She marked those down and then let out a huge yawn. "Sorry, it's been a very hectic few days. I can't remember the last time I slept."

"Oh my dear, I am so sorry," said Lady Hyacinth, rising at once from her chair. She closed the little book and blew out the candles on the candelabra. "Come, you can sleep in my bed. I'll be just across the hall in one of our guest bedrooms." She shook her head as Nikki started to object. "No, no arguing. You look absolutely dead tired.

Have a nice long sleep and we will tackle the rest of the book first thing in the morning."

Nikki was too tired to argue. She fell into the huge canopied bed and was asleep before Lady Hyacinth finished tucking her in.

# Chapter Three

Digging for Secrets

WHEN NIKKI WOKE the next morning she found that the skirt of her red silk gown had tangled itself around her head. When she finally managed to emerge from the layers of silk like a rumpled butterfly she found a long rip in the skirt from waist to hem. The dress was no longer wearable, and all she had on under it was her Westlake Debate Team T-shirt. She climbed with difficulty out of the huge, squishy feather bed and wandered around the immense bedroom, poking into chests and wardrobes. She felt a twinge of guilt at invading her hostess's privacy, but after travelling around the Realm for months with no extra clothes or possessions of her own she'd gotten used to scrounging and "borrowing" other people's stuff. Fuzz would be proud.

There were tons of silk and satin ball gowns in the wardrobes, but she didn't like being encased in layers of fabric. It was hard to make a quick getaway from the Rounders when you were wearing a ball gown. Finally at the back of one wardrobe she found a simple dress made of linen with a matching apron. It had grass and mud stains on the hem and she guessed that a servant had left it there. She breathed a sigh of relief as she put it on. It was much more comfortable than the red silk gown.

She padded barefoot across the plush carpet to the table they'd been sitting at the night before, only to find that the little book was gone. She was about to dash across the hall to the guestroom Lady Hyacinth was sleeping in when a thought occurred to her. She dropped to her knees next to the bed and peered underneath. There were nothing but dust bunnies on the carpet, but when she thrust her arm between the mattress and the bedsprings she found the book. Not a very original hiding place. She was surprised that someone as rich as Lady Hyacinth didn't have an iron safe or a locked treasury like the one up at Castle Cogent. She carried the book over to the table and sat down. Her parchment and quill and ink were still on the table. The morning sun was beginning to shine through the gauzy curtains of the floor-to-ceiling windows and there was plenty of light to read by.

As she scanned the strange symbols she realized she'd forgotten to look for prepositions the night before. The preposition 'to' was the third most common word in the English language and it was a conveniently short word. Plus she'd already identified the symbol for the letter 'T'. Yes, here was a likely candidate. A two-symbol word beginning with T. The symbol next to it looked like a crescent moon. She found the symbol on her parchment and wrote the letter "O" next to it.

That gave her ten letters identified. Seven she was fairly sure of and three that were pretty good guesses. There were twenty-six letters in the English alphabet, so she was nearly halfway there. A few letters such as Q, X, and Z were so rarely used that she could ignore them. She was extremely relieved that the code writer had kept the original spaces between words. When encoding a document it was much smarter to remove all the spaces and string the words together. That made it much harder to decode. She was also glad that the code writer hadn't done a shift cipher, where the letters were shifted over by a certain count. The most famous shift cipher was the Caesar Cipher, named for Julius Caesar, who'd used the shift cipher method in some of his military correspondence. She'd studied it in one of her computer science classes. In the Caesar Cipher each letter was shifted to the right by three. So the letter A became the letter D, and the letter B became the letter E. But she found no evidence of that kind of thing in the book. It was encoded with a direct symbol-to-letter substitution. Which was kind of strange, really. The code writer had gone to a lot of trouble to make up complicated symbols, but otherwise had done nothing else to disguise the original text. It gave the impression of someone who thought they were being clever but who obviously had no experience with ciphers.

Nikki kept at her decoding for another hour or so. Just as the sun came fully over the horizon she wrote the last decoded symbol on her parchment. She now had all the letters from A to Z and was just starting to write out the original text when the bedroom door creaked. She just had time to hide the book under her apron before the door swung open.

"Don't worry, my dear," said Lady Hyacinth. "It's just me." She was wearing a purple velvet dressing gown and leaning heavily on a cane. "It's an arthritis day," she said as she sat down at the table and hung her cane from the back of her chair. "I foolishly let the Count waltz me around the ballroom yesterday. I should have known better. Whenever I try to do the things I did in my youth my aching knees drag me back to reality." She pulled a roll of parchment out of the pocket of her robe, as well as another quill and ink pot. "I thought you might need these."

"Thanks," said Nikki, tearing off a piece of the parchment and flattening it out. "I have all of the symbols identified. Now I just need to write out the original text." She pulled the book out from under her apron. "I hope you don't mind me borrowing this dress. I found it in the back of a cupboard."

"You're welcome to it, my dear," said Lady Hyacinth. "I believe it belonged to one of the maids who helps with the flower arrangements.

That would explain the grass stains on the elbows. I'm sure we provided her with a new dress ages ago." She bent over the parchment Nikki had been writing on. "So clever of you, my dear," she said, examining the list of symbols. "Now that you've completed the hardest part why don't I help you with the rest. We can each take a page. We'll put the book here between us. You translate the left page and I'll take the right."

"Okay," said Nikki. She put the list of symbols between them and tore another piece off the scroll for Lady Hyacinth to write on.

The first few pages were slow going, but as they worked they started to memorize some of the more common symbols without even trying. By the time they were halfway through the small book they were writing furiously, as if they'd been fluent in the strange symbols all their lives.

"It must be about noon," said Nikki as she finally set her quill down and looked out the window. The sun was high in the sky and gardeners were busy trimming the grass on the immense lawn next to the mansion with long sickles.

"My dear, we need to discuss our results," Lady Hyacinth said firmly.

Nikki felt her shoulders hunch up to her ears and she continued looking out the window. It was a lovely day, with puffy white clouds in a clear blue sky and the sunlight shining on the Clearwater River.

"We need to discuss them *now*," said Lady Hyacinth, putting a hand on Nikki's shoulder and gently turning her around. "The first half of the book we can ignore for the moment. It might come in handy in the future, if any of the Knights of the Iron Fist are ever brought to trial. But their various recruiting tactics and drunken brawls are not of critical importance. But the second half . . ."

"Yes," said Nikki, wincing. "The second half. The dam."

Lady Hyacinth nodded, leafing through the pages of parchment they'd copied out. "I'd say these five pages are the most critical. They discuss the when and the how. The date of their planned sabotage is exactly one week from today. That much is clear. The how I don't entirely understand. There are many mentions of something called black powder. I am not familiar with this substance."

"I am," said Nikki quietly.

"The book says that there is a girl who knows how to make this black powder," said Lady Hyacinth. "It says that a Lurker observed her demonstrating this powder several months ago in Deceptionville. Apparently this powder is capable of creating a powerful explosion. Is this girl you?"

Nikki shook her head. "No. It's a friend of mine called Gwen. You probably know her. She's the daughter of Lady Ursula, the Duchess of Malaprop. She used to live with her mother at Muddled Manor, but she moved to Deceptionville and worked for a while in an alchemist shop run by a man named Avaricious. Gwen's an expert alchemist. She loves messing with chemicals and potions. She discovered how to make this black powder. She demonstrated it to me, Fuzz, and Athena when we were visiting her in Deceptionville."

"Of course!" exclaimed Lady Hyacinth. "Little Gwennie! Why I haven't seen her since she was twelve years old. Even back then she was always hiding out in the basement at Muddled Manor, mixing her potions. She would come to the dinner table with burns on her arms and half her lovely golden hair singed off. She was a sweet child though, despite her odd habits. I don't understand why she would create a powder capable of destroying Cogent Town."

"She wouldn't," said Nikki. "She wants to use her black powder for good. To make mining and tunnel-building easier. Just blow up the rock instead of hacking at it with pick axes. It would save thousands of men a great deal of hard, back-breaking labor. Unfortunately, the powder can also be used for evil things, such as blowing up Clearwater dam."

"But I don't really see how the Knights plan to carry out their sabotage of the dam," said Lady Hyacinth. "Little Gwennie isn't going to make a pile of this powder on command. Even if the Knights or that little rat Rufius order her to. And her family has nearly as much money as I do. I very much doubt that she'd be open to bribes. Though it might be prudent to convince her to hide away somewhere. For her own safety and the safety of Cogent Town."

"It's too late for that," said Nikki. "She was snatched by a Lurker from the Fox and Fig tavern several days ago. Fuzz and Athena are pretty sure that Rufius has her, we just don't know where."

Lady Hyacinth looked horrified. She began frantically leafing through the pages of parchment. "I don't see any mention of Gwen. Though if she was taken only days ago then this book won't help find her. I acquired it weeks ago." She drummed her fingers on the table. "Rufius has weaseled his way into Castle Cogent, but his real base of power is the Southern Castle. The Knights of the Iron Fist are quartered near there and they mainly stay down in the southern parts of the Realm, thank goodness. The King has so far refused to let them enter Cogent Town, but Rufius is wearing him down even on that score. Rufius might be keeping Gwen at the Southern Castle."

"I don't think so," said Nikki. "It would take too long to get her there, and then too long to get any black powder she is forced to make back up here to Cogent Town. I think . . ."

Nikki stopped talking as the door to the bedroom swung open. A maid in a neat blue linen dress came in. Nikki froze as she recognized Ava's sister. A wave of guilt washed over her. Her focus on decoding the little book had caused her to forget all about Ava's death in the flour mill.

Ava's sister approached the table and then paused, looking curiously at Nikki. "I can find you another gown, Miss," she said. "If you would like."

Nikki realized how strange it must look to the maid, to see her wearing a servant's linen dress. "Thank you," she said quickly. "But I am perfectly comfortable in this. My gown from last night has a large tear in it and I needed something to put on."

The maid went over to the canopied bed and retrieved the red silk ball gown. "Oh yes, Miss. This is quite a rip. All the way to the floor. I don't think my skill with a needle is up to the task. I'll have the dress sent to a seamstress we use in town. She's an expert at repairing silk."

Nikki cleared her throat. She could feel the words sticking in her throat, but she forced them out anyway. "I believe you have a sister who also works as a lady's maid. Her name is Ava."

The maid stared at her in surprise. "Why yes, Miss. She works in the house of the Duchess of Falsa. I don't get to see her often. The Duchess of Falsa lives near the Castle and we are on the outskirts of town here. How is it you know my sister?"

"I was a guest of the Duchess of Falsa," said Nikki, racking her brain for a believable lie. "Your sister helped me dress for one of the Duchess's parties. I . . . I am so sorry to have to tell you this, but I believe your sister has passed."

The maid frowned at her. "Passed, Miss? What do you mean?"

"I mean she may have passed away," said Nikki. "I believe she met with an accident of some kind. I don't know all the details."

A torrent of emotions passed across Ava's sister's face, from shock to disbelief to confusion. She dropped the red silk gown and it fell in a heap around her feet.

Lady Hyacinth rose from the table and forced the maid to sit down. She retrieved her cane from the back of her chair and hobbled over to a nearby cabinet. From the top drawer she pulled out a glass bottle and a brandy snifter. She poured out a generous helping and put the glass on the table in front of the maid. "Drink the whole thing, my dear," she said. "Brandy from the Popularnum vineyards. Strong stuff. It will calm your nerves."

Ava's sister took a small sip and then pushed the glass away. "I don't *want* my nerves calm," she said. "I want to know what happened to my sister."

Lady Hyacinth sat down and looked questioningly at Nikki.

Nikki debated telling Ava's sister the truth, but decided against it. The maid might spread the story of her sister's death in the flour mill to the other servants in the house, and that would probably lead to the Rounders paying the mansion a visit. "I'm sorry," she said. "I don't know anymore. I only overheard a brief conversation about it. Two servants of the Duchess of Falsa were talking about it."

Ava's sister jumped up from the table. "I need to talk to them. Right away. My lady, I will require a few days off."

Lady Hyacinth nodded. "Of course, my dear. Take as much time as you want. Take the carriage. If the coachman gives you any back talk tell him I order him to take you anywhere you want."

The maid gave a brief curtsy to Lady Hyacinth and ran from the room, hurriedly closing the door behind her.

"I'm sorry," said Nikki. "Maybe this wasn't the right time to tell her, but I just had to get it off my chest. And she has a right to know."

"Yes, she has a right to know," said Lady Hyacinth. "But maybe you should have told her the real story. You're not a talented liar, my dear."

"No, I'm not," said Nikki. "But it's a complicated story about fireworks, the King's Alchemist, men from the Mystic Mountains, an attack on the imps, and a flour mill."

"Do I need to know the real story?" asked Lady Hyacinth.

"Maybe," said Nikki. "It does tie in with your code book and the destruction of Clearwater dam. But do we really have time for long stories? It seems to me our first priority is to get Gwen back before she can be forced to make any more black powder."

"Yes, that is urgent," said Lady Hyacinth. "But we need a plan. It's no good rushing around blindly. I think we . . ."

Lady Hyacinth was interrupted by a knock on the bedroom door.

"Come in," called Lady Hyacinth.

A footman in midnight-blue livery and white silk stockings came in and bowed low. "My lady, I am very sorry to disturb you, but two men have appeared at the front door and they insist on speaking to you." He paused, a grimace passing across his face. "They are most definitely *not* the type of person your ladyship usually socializes with. So I ordered them to wait outside. I have three footmen and two grooms guarding them."

"My goodness!" said Lady Hyacinth. "Was that really necessary?"

"They were being overly insistent, my lady. They tried to force their way through the front door."

"Are they armed?" asked Lady Hyacinth.

"No, my lady. But they are quite rough looking."

"Well," said Lady Hyacinth. "This is most unusual, but I suppose the easiest way to get rid of them is for me to see them. Have them brought up here. My arthritis is acting up today and I'm not ready to face the stairs yet. Bring their guards too."

The footman bowed and left.

"My dear, you had better hide," said Lady Hyacinth. "These men might recognize you from your posters."

"I'll go across the hall and hide in one of your guest rooms," said Nikki, gathering up the code book and the pages of parchment. "I'll take these with me, just in case."

"No, I want you to hear what they have to say," said Lady Hyacinth. "Most likely it's just a couple of ruffians wanting a handout. But you never know. They may have information to pass along to me about the recent troubles in the Realm. It's well known in town that I am sympathetic to the imps. People who share my sympathies will sometimes bring me news of Rufius and his plots. Go hide in that wardrobe over there. You'll be near enough to hear what they have to say."

Nikki took the code book and the parchments with her and climbed into the wardrobe next to the canopied bed. It was full of silk gowns hanging from an iron rod. She shoved the gowns over to one side and closed the door. She didn't have long to wait. She heard the bedroom door open again and the sounds of a scuffle filled the room.

"I insist that these servants unhand me, my lady," said a deep voice. "I am a respectable citizen of the Realm. A master stonemason by trade. I am not some street criminal, to be treated in this disrespectful manner."

Inside the wardrobe Nikki's mouth fell open in surprise and she nearly dropped the code book. She recognized the voice at once. It was Darius.

"You have my permission to unhand him," said Lady Hyacinth. "But stay close in case he becomes unruly."

"What about this other one, my lady?" asked one of the footmen. "He won't stop squirming. I'm afraid he might try to do your ladyship harm."

"I ain't gonna hurt the old lady," snarled a rough, uneducated voice. "I just don't likes being treated like some stray dog off the street."

Nikki closed her eyes, trying to stir her memory. She recognized the voice but couldn't put a name to it.

"You may let him go also," said Lady Hyacinth. "You seem familiar, young man. Haven't I seen you up at Castle Cogent, scurrying behind Geber, the King's Alchemist?"

Of course, Nikki thought. It was Sander. Geber's assistant.

"Don't know about no scurrying," Sander said resentfully. "I has a respectable position in old Geber's laboratories. In D-ville and up at the Castle. I helps him with his potions and stuff."

"Well, that's very nice for you, I'm sure," said Lady Hyacinth. "Now, what is it you two want? Out with it. I have a busy day today."

There was a long silence. Finally Darius spoke. "We're looking for a friend of ours. We traced her to the mansion of the Duchess of Falsa, and we have reason to believe she may have come here on the advice of one of the Duchess's servants."

"Oh?" said Lady Hyacinth. "And who is this friend of yours?"

"She goes by the name of Nikki," said Darius. "But she may be using a false name. The Rounders have been looking hard for her all over town. She may be in disguise as well."

"My goodness," said Lady Hyacinth. "How very mysterious. If this Nikki person is trying so hard to hide her identity what makes you think she'll want to see you?"

There was another long silence.

Finally Darius spoke reluctantly. "She may not want to, to be honest. We have a strong difference of opinion on a certain subject. But even so I need to find her. She may be a great help in finding the woman I love."

"A mystery and a love story," said Lady Hyacinth. "This gets more entertaining by the minute."

"I am not here for your ladyship's amusement," snapped Darius. "The woman I love is in great danger and I *must* find her. She is a noblewoman like yourself, so I thought your ladyship might be willing to help."

"She wouldn't happen to be Gwendolyn, Lady Ursula's daughter, would she?" asked Lady Hyacinth.

"Yes, she is," said Darius, sounding surprised. "That was a very lucky guess on the part of your ladyship."

"Not really," said Lady Hyacinth. "I've recently heard some disturbing news about little Gwennie. But I'm afraid I don't know where she is."

"But Nikki, the girl I am looking for, she might know," said Darius. "If she is here I beseech your ladyship to tell me. I am not requesting money from your ladyship. Nor do I need men from your staff. I have brought help of my own. They are friends of Gwendolyn and are eager to help me with a rescue mission. They are waiting outside in your rose garden."

"In my rose garden?" asked Lady Hyacinth. "Who are they? Soldiers? Mercenaries?"

"They are pirates from the southern coast," said Darius.

"I have pirates in my rose garden?" asked Lady Hyacinth in astonishment.

"Griff!" Nikki exclaimed, bursting from her hiding place. "Is her whole crew here?"

Sander was the first to recover from Nikki's sudden appearance. "Hello, Miss," he said. "Ya probably remembers me from D-ville. I know I didn't treat ya real nice-like when we first met. But I did save ya from that Lurker in the Wolf's Head tavern."

"Yes, you did," said Nikki thoughtfully. She went up to Sander and stared closely at him. She'd never really trusted him, and she still didn't. "Why are you here Sander?"

Sander shrugged. "I guess I just want ta make up for some of me past mistakes, that's all. Working for old Geber is a good job, but he does lots of bad stuff. Down in D-ville he was in with Fortuna, making potions for her. Some of them potions had real nasty side-effects, like burns on people's faces. Geber didn't care. He was just in it for the money. And lately up at the castle he's been hanging around with the little pimple Rufius. Them two been hatching schemes. No good'll come of it. I been having nightmares, and I been feeling guilty all the time. Can't work for him no more. And I feel like maybe I should help make things right, if I can."

"How exactly would you do that?" asked Nikki.

Sander turned red and stared at the floor. "Don't really know. I was hoping maybe you'd have some ideas."

Nikki crossed her arms and stared at him, thinking. Nobody knew Geber was dead. Someone like Sander, who had access to Geber's laboratory up at Castle Cogent, could be very useful. "Would you be willing to search Geber's laboratory?" she asked him.

"Um, I guess so," said Sander. "What would I look for?"

"Notes, letters, parchments, scrolls," said Nikki. "Any kind of written material. It's possible that Geber has been writing down some of Rufius's plans. Or maybe keeping letters he's sent. Gather up anything you can find and bring it to the house of the Prince of Physics here in town."

"Okay," said Sander. "I thinks I can do that. Doubt anyone will notice. Nobody but me and old Geber ever go into his laboratory. The servants and guards up at the castle think old Geber's a magician and that he'll put a spell on them. Turn them into spotted toads if they sets a foot into his quarters. But just to be safe maybe I should wait until dark. Less people around to spot me."

"No, go right now," said Nikki. "It's urgent." Once people learned of Geber's death the Rounders or the castle guards would search Geber's laboratory, or lock it and put a guard on it.

Sander looked a bit startled at the sudden order, but he gave her an ironic little salute and promptly left the room, two footmen following him closely.

"Will you come outside, Miss?" asked Darius. "Griff will want to talk to you. Most of her crew are here as well. They have news for you about the battle of ImpHaven, but I'll let Griff tell you the details."

"I don't think . . ." began Lady Hyacinth.

"It's okay," said Nikki, handing her the code book and parchments. "They're old friends." She hurriedly put on the red silk shoes from the night before and followed Darius out of the bedroom and down the stairs, the footmen and grooms trailing in their wake.

Darius didn't say a word as he led her out the front entrance of the mansion, past several carriages leftover from last night's party and across the immense lawn leading to the river. There was a strong smell of cut grass, though the gardeners with the lawn shears had disappeared. The rose garden was at the far edge of the lawn, overlooking the river. As they approached Nikki could see that the garden was enclosed by a white picket fence taller than Darius.

Massive vines of red and pink roses hung from the fence, swaying in the morning breeze. As they passed through a gap in the roses a young man suddenly stepped in front of them. He was dressed in a white and blue striped shirt and grimy canvas trousers that stank of fish.

Nikki recognized him from her time spent on Griff's ship. She couldn't remember his name so she just gave him a small wave. The sailor grinned at her and gestured for them to follow him. The garden was laid out in concentric circles of rose bushes. They followed the sailor through a circle of yellow roses, then one of white, then two of salmon pink before finally arriving at the center of the garden where a motley group of sailors was sitting on white marble benches surrounding a splashing fountain. Several of them had taken off their boots and were cooling their feet in the water.

"Griff!" exclaimed Nikki, running up to the tall pirate in her dashing leather coat and knee-high boots.

Griff gave her a cheerful thump on the back and looked her up and down. "You look a bit worse for wear, young codfish," she said, pointing at Nikki's chin.

Nikki felt along her chin. Several tender lumps lined her jaw, thanks to the explosion at the flour mill. She realized they must have turned purple overnight. She must look like quite a spectacle. "I'm fine," she said quickly. She looked around at the sailors. "Where's Posie? And Tarn?"

"Posie stayed on board the ship," said Griff. "It's tied up at a dock in Kingston harbor. Someone needed to watch over it and Posie offered. She wasn't up to a long journey by land. She's getting a bit too old to be a ship's cook, but she won't admit it. She stays mostly in her cabin nowadays and feeds pieces of codfish to stray cats." A brief cloud of anger passed over her sunburned face. "Tarn's dead. Killed in the attack on ImpHaven."

"Oh," said Nikki. "Yes, of course. I knew that. Athena told me.

I'm sorry."

Griff nodded sadly. "He was about as pleasant as a rabid dog, but despite that he's missed. He was a part of the crew for a long time, and a better codfish spotter never sailed the southern ocean. He showed remarkable bravery in ImpHaven, at times single-handedly facing down armed knights. Never thought of him as the brave type, but I think defending his homeland and his own people made a difference."

"I suppose ImpHaven's occupied territory now", said Nikki sadly. "The Knights of the Iron Fist are probably lording it up in Athena's mother's house and breaking all her china teacups."

"Nope," said Griff. "I think occupying ImpHaven was Rufius's original plan, but he didn't reckon with the laziness of mercenaries. Because that's exactly what the Knights of the Iron Fist are. Paid fighters. They like a bit of sword play, a bit of excitement, and then they like to get paid so they can spend their days drinking ale and gambling. Rufius did try to rally them to attack Kingston and the Southern Castle as well as occupying ImpHaven, but that was way too much work for them. The Prince of Physics gathered some of his men as well as the guards at the Southern Castle still loyal to the King and they chased the Knights out of Kingston and down the coast."

"So that's why Rufius has suddenly appeared here, back in Cogent Town," said Nikki.

Griff nodded. "Yep. The little snot is finding that power grabs aren't quite as easy as he imagined. My guess is that he's changed his plans. He was trying to build a base of power at the Southern Castle, but when that fell through he shifted his focus to Castle Cogent. It's the main seat of power in the Realm. He thinks that if he can control or even kill the King then the whole Realm will automatically obey him. I think he's wrong about that, but we shall see. The ace up his sleeve is all the money he's been throwing around. I can't think where he gets it all from. It's not family money. His parents are just cheese mongers from D-ville."

"It's from the castle treasury," said Nikki. "Rufius and Geber, the King's alchemist, have been minting fake coins. Passing tin off as gold. They've probably also been stealing actual gold from the treasury."

Griff raised an eyebrow. "You *have* been busy, young flounder. That's a bit of information I think the citizens of the Realm should be told. That's their tax money Rufius is stealing. The King should be told too, of course, though that might be difficult. From what I hear he's under Rufius's thumb."

"Enough!" Darius suddenly shouted, his face red with anger. "You two can spend entire days discussing politics and plans for all I care, *after* we've rescued Gwen."

"There are many people at risk in the Realm right now, stonemason," said Griff coldly. "She's just one person."

"That's true," said Nikki, stepping in front of Darius, who looked about to throw a punch at the pirate. "But rescuing Gwen *does* need to be a priority. For other reasons besides Darius's romantic impulses." She glanced around at the sailors lounging around the fountain. She recognized most of their faces, but didn't really know any of them well. It was possible one of them was a spy, bribed by Rufius to report the pirates' movements to him. She decided it wasn't a good idea to discuss Gwen's black powder experiments in front of such a large group.

"Why don't you and I go inside?" Nikki suggested. "I'll ask Lady Hyacinth to send some food out here for your crew."

"Hmm," said Griff. "Not one of your better ideas young starfish. Us pirates have never gotten along well with the nobility. They seem to think we're thieves. We might occasionally pick up a few trinkets from sunken vessels, and some have accused us of plundering the trading ports in the Southern Isles, but mostly we spend our days as honest fishers of the noble cod. And the nobility also say we stink, which I agree is hard to argue with. I throw my men overboard now and then for a little swim in the sea, but the smell of codfish oil never washes away."

"Don't worry," said Nikki. "Lady Hyacinth is very nice. And she's a long-time friend of Fuzz and Athena. But you're right. It would be better if your crew stayed out here in the garden."

Griff still looked skeptical, but she nodded. "You lot stay here and stay out of trouble," she yelled at the sailors. "No going into the house. We'll send some grub out to you. And even some ale if you behave yourselves."

Darius started to follow Griff and Nikki out of the rose garden, but Griff held up a hand. "You stay here too," she said. "You're in a stormy mood and I want to leave this estate with all my limbs still attached. Your temper is likely to get the dogs sicked on us. The nobility around these parts are well-known to breed blood-hungry mastiffs."

Darius glared at her, but Griff glared back until the stonemason finally shrugged in annoyance and plunked down on a bench.

# Chapter Four

## Weakness

GRIFF BANGED HER empty mug of ale down on the table in Lady Hyacinth's bedroom with a satisfied sigh. "Wonderful stuff. Haven't had this particular brew before."

"It's our own home recipe," said Lady Hyacinth, primly sipping from her mug. "We have a brewery behind the stables."

Nikki wrinkled her nose. She hated the smell of beer and ale. Lady Hyacinth had offered her a mug, but she politely declined. She knew it was common for kids to drink ale in the Realm, but it was still unnerving when an adult offered her some. The adults here weren't trying to get her drunk, it was just that ale was safer to drink than water. Sewage was dumped straight into the creeks and rivers and there were no water purification systems in the Realm. The only attempt to get clean drinking water that she'd seen was a very basic sand-filtering system at the Prince of Physics' estate in Kingston. A sand-filter could trap pieces of deer or duck poop floating in the water, but all the nasty bacteria which caused diseases like cholera and dysentery were still swimming merrily around in your glass of drinking water. Distillation could remove bacteria from water by heating it until it turned to steam and then letting it cool back into water. But she doubted that anyone in the Realm except maybe very educated people like Geber used distillation. Fortunately apple juice was very popular in the Realm. She stuck to that or milk when she could get it, or tea if the water had been boiled.

"Right," said Griff. "Let's get down to it. You started to tell us something about tunnels."

"Yes," said Lady Hyacinth, leafing through the pieces of parchment that she and Nikki had decoded. "It's here on this page. The code book was a bit smudged in this part, so I'm not sure exactly what it was trying to say. But as near as I can make out it's referring to the Long Tombs."

"The what?" asked Griff with a startled expression.

"The Long Tombs," repeated Lady Hyacinth. "They're tunnels in the rocky hills not far from here. Near the start of the road to Freibergen. They're called the Long Tombs because of all the cave-ins during their construction. It was brutal work. The men had to use pick-axes to cut through solid granite. But the rock was laced with seams of weaker sandstone, which would collapse on top of their heads. It wasn't possible to clear some of the biggest piles of rubble, so they would just leave the bodies buried there. Not many people in Cogent Town know about the Long Tombs. They were dug long ago and they caused so many deaths that people just wanted to forget about them. The only reason I know about them is because some of my ancestors paid for their construction. They were built at the same time as the Clearwater dam. They're access tunnels for the dam."

Lady Hyacinth picked up a quill and drew a quick sketch of a waterwheel on a blank piece of parchment. "Centuries ago there were some very talented engineers in the Realm. They knew a great deal more about water power than we know today. After the Clearwater dam was built they added these tunnels. And at the end of the tunnels they constructed huge waterwheels which could stand tremendous force. They were much larger than the small wheels we use today for irrigating fields. They used the crushing force of water released via spillways next to the dam to grind massive amounts of grain. This created much more flour than the Realm could consume and we became exporters of flour to other lands. My ancestors became extremely wealthy from these exports."

Griff glanced briefly at the sketch of tunnels and waterwheels that Lady Hyacinth had drawn. She shrugged. "Interesting history lesson, but not terribly useful that I can see."

"Not very useful to us, maybe," replied Lady Hyacinth, "but very useful to Rufius. According to this code book which our young friend here has deciphered, Rufius plans to use these tunnels to destroy much of Cogent Town. The book says his plan is to place black powder in large heaps at certain places in the Long Tombs where the rock walls are weak and very close to the dam. This black powder creates an explosion when lit which could be strong enough to destroy the dam. The entire body of water behind the dam will come crashing into Cogent Town. My guess is only Castle Cogent will survive. It's the only high place in town. Everything else, houses, people, animals will be washed away. The death and destruction will be enormous, and Rufius plans to use the ensuing chaos to take power in the Realm. He already has the King's trust, and our dear King is just not good in a crisis. He'll be only too happy to turn over the reins of power to the young advisor who's been whispering compliments into his ear for much of this year."

"Hmm," said Griff, taking another look at the sketch. "What's black powder?"

"Remember when an entire wall of the Southern Castle was destroyed by an explosion?" asked Nikki.

"Sure," said Griff. "We weren't in Kingston at the time, but everyone up and down the southern coast heard about that. Lots of rumors flew around about the cause, but I never heard any reliable information about it."

"I'm sure Rufius ordered the soldiers at the Southern Castle not to talk about it," said Nikki. "It was black powder that caused the explosion."

Griff glanced up at her, and it was the first time Nikki had ever seen fear in the pirate's eyes.

Griff sat back in her chair, rubbing her temples as if she had a headache. "Where's Rufius getting this stuff from? This powder?"

"From a friend of mine," said Nikki. "A girl a few years older than me called Gwen. She's an expert alchemist. Probably even more knowledgeable than Geber, the King's alchemist. She's not making this powder voluntarily. She was taken from the Fox and Fig tavern here in Cogent Town not long ago. A Lurker grabbed her. I saw it happen, and I think she was taken to Rufius. He's going to try and force her to make more of the black powder. I'm sure of it. They'll need a lot to bring down the dam, and I don't think Gwen ever made very much of it. She gave me, Fuzz, and Athena a small demonstration of it when she was living in Deceptionville, but she'd only made a handful of the powder. Rufius will need barrels full of it."

"How long does it take to make?" asked Griff.

"I'm not sure," said Nikki, frowning. She knew that old-fashioned versions of gunpowder were made from sulfur, charcoal, and potassium nitrate. Charcoal was fairly easy to make by heating wood in a furnace where most of the air had been drawn out. And the Realm probably had stockpiles of sulfur. Avaricious had large stores of it in his shop in Deceptionville, and he was pals with Rufius. But the potassium nitrate would slow things down. In her world back home there were modern ways of making it, but here in the Realm they probably relied on the smelly and slow process of fermenting urine. Even if they collected it from cows and horses as well as people it would take time to get enough. And the collection process would start people asking questions. Someone running up with a bucket every time a horse stopped to pee in the street would definitely catch people's attention. "It depends," she finally said. "If Rufius has the necessary ingredients already on hand then it would only take a couple of hours to make the final powder. But he would still need an expert like Gwen to do the mixing. The ingredients have to be combined in certain ratios. If he doesn't have the ingredients yet then it could take weeks."

"Well," said Griff. "I think we should go by the worst-case scenario and assume time is short. I say we head for the Long Tombs right now and check things out. We'll take a few of my men with us for protection, but I'll need to leave the rest of my crew in the rose garden. A few of us won't cause much disturbance, but a large band of pirates travelling through the countryside will definitely have the neighborhood calling for the Rounders. We had to travel in small groups from Kingston and meet up here in Cogent Town so as not to attraction attention."

"That's fine," said Lady Hyacinth. "Pirates can't do any more damage to my roses than my neighbor's steer did. It got loose from its pen last year and rampaged through my yellow roses, tore through the climbing tea-rose vines, and charged straight into the French windows on the ground floor of this house. I was having a tea party near the windows at the time and Lord Merryton nearly got gored by its horns. Fortunately the only thing the steer managed to spear was a cherry tart." She rose from her chair and retrieved her cane. "I'll just pop down to the kitchen and have a quiet word with the cook. She's a sensible woman who can keep her mouth shut. She'll see to it that food is sent out to your crew without the rest of the household noticing. And your crew can sleep in the hay barn. It's shut until winter, so no one should notice overnight visitors."

NIKKI WINCED AS she pulled off the sturdy boots Lady Hyacinth had given her. They were much better for walking than the red silk shoes she'd had on, but her feet weren't used to them and they were giving her blisters. She lifted the skirt of her borrowed dress and waded out into the ice-cold water of the Clearwater River. The water was so cold that her legs soon turned numb, but at least her blisters stopped stinging. Tiny silver minnows swam in circles around her legs and river mud gushed between her toes. On the opposite bank a heron was perched on a log, watching the water intently for its next meal.

"Be careful there, young codfish," Griff called out. "The current here is very strong."

Nikki waved at her and waded back to the small sandy beach they had chosen as a rest stop.

Griff, Darius, and three pirates were sitting on boulders, munching on bread and chunks of cheese. Darius handed Nikki bread and cheese from his rucksack and they all sat quietly eating. An owl hooted nearby as the dusk closed in.

Nikki shivered and pulled a wool sweater out of the rucksack Lady Hyacinth had given her. "How much farther is it?" she asked.

Griff pulled a piece of parchment out of her coat pocket. Lady Hyacinth had drawn a rough sketch of the location of the Long Tombs. Their entrance was only five miles from Lady Hyacinth's estate, but the walk had been very steep, going straight up into the rocky hills toward the source of the Clearwater River.

"We should be only a hundred paces or so from the entrance to the main tunnel," said Griff. "We'll wait here until dark. I've no idea if Rufius has left any guards nearby, but better to avoid any encounters if possible. If we do come across trouble me and my boys will fight them off." She fixed Darius with a stern eye. "You take the young codfish and hide in the woods. If we don't return make your way back to the rose garden."

Darius looked like he was about to object, but Griff stared him down.

Nikki pulled her boots back on. She left the river mud on her feet, hoping it might ease her blisters. She fervently hoped they wouldn't come across any guards. The last thing she wanted was to travel with only Darius for company. She'd been surprised when Griff had chosen him to come with them to the dam, but Griff had pointed out that he was a master stonemason and could be of use in examining the structure of the dam.

When Nikki had first met Darius she'd thought that he was kind of dull, but nice enough. But ever since learning that he was a Remover who wanted all the imps kicked out of the Realm she couldn't stand to be around him. It was so strange, as if he were two people. When they'd rescued Athena's Aunt Gertie from the dungeon of the Southern Castle Darius had carried the old imp on his back, even when she'd threatened to hit him with her cane. Nikki was having a hard time understanding his split personality on the imp issue. It reminded her of the musical *South Pacific*, which was one of her mother's favorites. Her mother played it all the time when she was making dinner. The musical had a famous song called *You've Got to be Carefully Taught*. The song was about racism, and how young children had to be taught by their parents to be racist. To hate and fear people who were different from them. Nikki had always thought that the song wasn't entirely correct. Some people just seemed to be born with a strong dislike of anyone different from themselves. It seemed to be an instinctive fear response which was stronger in some people than in others. People with this strong fear response were often more rigid, and craved certainty and sameness more than other people. Nikki supposed that Darius could have been taught to hate the imps by his parents, but somehow she felt that his bigotry stemmed more from having this rigid and inflexible type of personality.

Back at the mansion of the Prince of Physics Fuzz and Athena had seemed willing to work with Darius as an ally. Reluctant, but willing. But Nikki was having a hard time doing the same. Maybe it was because Fuzz and Athena were older and better at compromising. After decades as the King's emissaries they undoubtedly had lots of experience with politics and compromises and working with people they didn't agree with, or even like. She looked up and found Darius watching her, a knowing glance in his eyes, as if he knew what she was thinking. Nikki twisted around on the boulder she was perched on so that her back was to him. She knew Gwen had a crush on him, but it would never have worked out. They made a completely incompatible couple. Gwen was innovative and creative and adaptable. Everything that Darius was not.

Nikki gave an irritated shake of her head. She had more important things to focus on than the romantic trials of Gwen and Darius. She slid off the boulder and walked to the water's edge, staring upriver. She could just make out the looming shape of the Clearwater dam. It was difficult from this distance to make out any details. She needed a closer look.

They waited on the little beach for an hour until the sun had completely disappeared and stars began to appear in the midnight-blue sky. Griff silently stood up and motioned them to follow her. She led them along the river for a while, then suddenly turned away from the water, pushing through a thicket of alders bordering a barely noticeable path. Once past the thicket the path turned rocky and very steep. They soon had to crawl, pulling themselves along with their hands.

Nikki was last in line and small pebbles dislodged by the others kept bouncing down on her head. The night was very dark and she had crawled several feet inside a tunnel before even realizing she was no longer outside. She cautiously got to her feet, holding her hands up to keep from hitting her head on the ceiling. She found that she could stand upright, and that she could reach both sides of the tunnel with her fingertips. The rock walls were smooth and damp. Her boots splashed in a rivulet of water trickling along the tunnel floor. No one spoke, but she could hear their footsteps moving away from her. She hurried to catch up, nearly bumping into the pirate in front of her.

They wound up hill in the pitch darkness for a long time. Every twenty yards or so the wet floor of the tunnel changed to steep steps. Then another flat stretch where they could catch their breath, then steep steps again.

Nikki was gasping for breath by the time Griff called for a halt.

A match flared and Griff's shadow flickered on the tunnel wall.

"There's a fork up ahead," Griff said quietly, looking down at Lady Hyacinth's map. "We take the left path, then soon after there's another fork and we take the right-hand path. Then we should be close to the old waterwheels." She blew out her match and continued onwards.

Nikki felt the opening before she saw it. A cold wind had entered the tunnel after the second fork and it was blowing her hair back from her face. She followed the others through a break in the rock wall and out onto a narrow ledge. The full moon had risen and it shone brightly on the rushing river. Nikki stifled a gasp as she looked up. They were right below the dam. Its immense rock walls curved up and away from them in a semi-circle, towering high above like something built by giants. From its shape Nikki could tell that it was an arch-gravity dam, with a parabolic shape which helped direct the immense load from the water toward the sides of the arch. Hydrostatic pressure redirected some of the force of the water towards the rock walls and helped to strengthen the dam and hold it in place. The weak points for this type of dam would be at the top of its spillways. She could hear one rushing somewhere behind her and she could see another one across the river. It was a narrow channel running alongside the dam, white with foam from the speed of the water flowing down it. Spillways were safety valves. Meant to channel excess water if the dam ever overflowed. A spillway started at the top of the dam, below water level. It had a gate which was normally kept closed, but could be opened in case the water level behind the dam was getting too high. It was these spillway gates which were the weak point. They were much weaker than the body of the dam. If they ruptured a huge amount of uncontrolled water would rush down, wearing away the sides of the dam and eventually causing the whole structure to collapse. It was at the top of the spillways where Rufius would place his barrels of black powder, if he succeeded in creating enough.

"Let's go to the top," Nikki called to Griff.

Griff cupped her ear and shook her head. The roar of the nearby spillway made talking impossible.

Nikki waved at the rest of them to follow her and went back through the opening into the tunnel. Another hour of rough climbing brought them to the top of the dam. A walkway of granite blocks about ten feet wide curved around the top, providing a vertigo-inducing view down to the base of the dam hundreds of feet below. One of Griff's crew took a quick look over the edge and abruptly sat down, his head in his hands.

Nikki carefully got down on her hands and knees and peered over the edge. They were directly above the right-hand spillway. She could see a fast stream of water pouring out of its gate. That probably meant that the water level was a bit too high and the gate had been opened slightly to lower the reservoir. She crawled to the other side of the walkway and peered down at the lake created by the dam. It looked quite full. The water level was only about ten feet below the walkway. The artificial lake stretched far away into the darkness. She couldn't tell exactly how big it was, but it was more than enough water to destroy Cogent Town if it all came crashing through the spillways at once.

Darius, who was laying on his stomach and peering down at the spillway gate, motioned Nikki and Griff over. "The stonework is starting to fail," he said, pointing down at a long jagged crack which started at the gate and stretched across the face of the dam. "You can see where they've patched it with mortar and tar." He heaved his broad shoulders over the edge to get a better look. "Some of that tar looks decades old. It's gone dry and useless. The patchwork is holding, for now. I don't see any water leaking from the crack, just from the gate. But I'd say there hasn't been any maintenance done on this crack for many years. This would be the perfect spot for Rufius to choose."

Nikki stretched farther over the edge, feeling Griff grab onto her wool sweater.

"Hold up there young flounder," said Griff. "Throwing yourself over the edge isn't going to help anyone."

"I just wanted a closer look," said Nikki, inching backwards and sitting up. "I don't think Rufius will place the black powder here. Not if he has anyone with him who understands engineering or construction. Just look at the immense size of the granite blocks up here. It's true that the crack is a weak spot, but I very much doubt that Rufius will be able to make so much powder that it will destroy even one of these blocks. I think we should take a look at the old waterwheel tunnels that Lady Hyacinth mentioned."

Griff nodded and called to her crew. They headed back along the walkway, the pirate with vertigo following behind on his hands and knees. Nikki was in the lead and she purposely went past the tunnel they'd come up in. Instead she bent low to the ground, trying to spot footprints in the muddy soil next to the dam. There were several trails leading away from the walkway, hacked through the thick under-brush. It took more than an hour of searching, but Nikki finally found what she was looking for.

"Over here," she called, waiting for the rest to catch up with her. When Griff appeared Nikki pointed at the ground.

Griff lit a match and bent down. "Boot prints," she said. "Several different types, I think. We haven't seen hide nor hair of any guards. These could just have been made by the blokes who work at the dam."

"Maybe," said Nikki. "But let's see where they go." She led the way, squinting down at the ground. The boot prints were faintly visible in the moonlight. The prints meandered through the forest and led to several dead ends and a lot of backtracking, as if the people who'd made the footprints didn't know exactly where they were going. But eventually the footprints led to an ancient wooden shed half-hidden by pine branches, its sides rotted with termite holes. Nikki slid through the half-open door and felt one foot step into nothingness. Griff grabbed her just in time.

"Thanks," Nikki gasped, her knees shaking as she stared down into the black depths of the hole she'd nearly fallen into. It was about three feet wide and went straight down into the earth.

Griff knelt beside her on the ground and lit a match, peering into the hole. "Can't see the bottom," she said. "There's iron rungs on the side. Kind of like a ladder. There's fresh mud on the top rungs, so somebody's been here recently." She motioned to her crew. "You three stay up here and keep watch."

Griff started down the rusty iron ladder and Darius followed. They had disappeared down into the darkness before Nikki finally pulled herself together enough to follow. She gingerly eased herself down into the hole, her hands still shaking. It soon became pitch black. She couldn't even see the iron rungs inches from her nose. Many of the rungs were loose, or even missing. Nikki had climbed down into the hole about fifty feet when she suddenly realized that she couldn't feel the next rung with her feet. She stretched out full length, hanging from one hand, but still nothing. In desperation she pulled herself back up and hung there, trying not to panic. The other two had gotten past the gap somehow. It had to be their height, she realized. They were taller than she was. Darius was more than a foot taller, but Griff was only about seven inches taller. So the next rung down was only seven inches past where she could reach. Holding tight with one hand she awkwardly pulled off her rucksack. The straps were fastened with heavy iron buckles. Unfastening a buckle in the dark with one hand seemed to take forever, but eventually she managed it. She looped the strap around the rung she was holding onto and re-fastened the buckle. Then taking a deep breath she slowly released both hands from the rung until she was hanging from the rucksack. She inched down it, her feet swinging. Far below she heard Griff calling to her. She was about to give up and wait for someone to climb back up and rescue her, when her foot hit something. She eased her toes onto it and tested its strength. It held.

"What took you so long?" Griff asked as Nikki climbed off the last rung and joined them at the bottom of the hole. "Are you all right?"

Nikki waved away the lit match that Griff was holding up to her face. "I'm fine. It was just an awkward climb. So, we've found another tunnel."

"Yep," said Griff. "Hang on a second." A match flared and a strong smell of pitch filled the air. Griff held a flaming torch above her head. "Easier than lighting matches all the time."

Nikki peered around, blinking at the bright light of the torch. They were in a kind of round chamber, with only one tunnel branching off of it. They started down it, only going a few feet before realizing that they must be very close to the spillway. Hundreds of tiny cracks in the stone walls were leaking. Water streamed down the walls and ran ankle-deep along the ground. The only reason the tunnel wasn't filling up with water was because it slanted steeply downhill. As they went lower down the leaks in the walls grew bigger and the water surged up to their knees.

"I don't think we should go much farther," said Darius, picking a soaking-wet Nikki up off the ground and standing her upright. The force of the water had knocked her off her feet.

"We don't have to," said Griff, holding her torch up to a spot on the wall. The flame shone on a large white X written in chalk. Griff put her hand on the wall next to it. "You can feel it, the force of the water."

Nikki put her hand on the wall. The stone was vibrating rapidly. When she put her ear next to the X she could hear a rushing sound. "This must be the weak spot," she said. "They're probably going to stuff the black powder into this large crack next to the X."

Darius took the torch from Griff and shone it into the crack. "The crack's dry, but it goes deep into the wall. I'd guess there's only about a foot or two of stone wall between the end of this crack and the spillway." He took a small hammer out of his rucksack and gently pinged on the wall around the crack, putting his ear to the stone after each ping. "Yes. The wall here is very thin. Whoever carved this tunnel originally didn't leave the outer wall thick enough, and it's probably worn away even more over the years. It's nothing but luck that the tunnel hasn't collapsed yet, even without black powder. If they open up the spillway gate to maximum, and destroy this tunnel at the same time that would severely weaken the dam. They wouldn't have to blow up the big granite blocks on top of the dam. Just sending the entire reservoir of water rushing down this side all at once would be enough to destabilize the whole structure. The dam might not collapse immediately, but all that water eating away at the hillside would bring it down pretty quickly. I'd guess it would only take a couple of days at the most."

"So we might have time to evacuate the town," said Griff. "That's good news, at least."

Darius shook his head. "I wouldn't count on that. It would be much better to prevent them from using the black powder in the first place. People frequently resist evacuating. Especially if they have a home or a shop they want to protect. My home village had a flash flood a few years ago and many lives were lost because people wouldn't abandon their homes or their farm animals. And besides, the people of Cogent Town won't listen to you or me. If we ran around town yelling for people to leave their houses they'd just think we were kooks and ignore us."

"Lady Hyacinth may be able to help with that," said Griff. "People here tend to follow the lead of the nobility in times of trouble. Down south in Kingston the townsfolk generally follow the Prince of Physics. He's seen as a kind of local ruler even though he rejects the idea that he has any official authority. But up here people defer to the courtiers and the nobles. If Lady Hyacinth ordered the townsfolk to evacuate they might do it."

"Then let's get out of here and go talk to her about it," said Nikki, her teeth chattering as she tried to keep her balance in the rushing water swirling around her knees. "If we hurry we can make it back before I freeze to death."

# Chapter Five

## Surrounded

NIKKI WAS THE last to climb out of the hole. On the climb up Darius pulled her past the gap in the rungs and retrieved her rucksack from the rung it was still buckled to. Nikki waited for Griff and Darius to leave the shed and then closed the door, careful to avoid the edge of the hole. She stripped off her soaking-wet clothes and pulled on a linen shirt and a heavy wool sweater which had been tucked down at the bottom of her pack. Griff had given her a spare pair of trousers from her own pack. Griff's trousers were too big, but by rolling up the pant legs and twisting her Westlake Debate Team T-shirt into a belt Nikki managed to keep them from falling down.

As she stepped out of the shed a shrieking wind whistled through the pines. The bitter cold of the night made her shiver even with the heavy wool sweater. She felt a sudden longing for home and a warm bowl of her mother's carrot soup. Not long now, she told herself. She had a feeling that one way or another things were starting to come to a head in the Realm. Either their fight against Rufius would be successful, or, well, best not to think too hard about the alternative.

"Hurry up, young codfish," said Griff. "We're all looking forward to a mug of ale and the warm fire of Lady Hyacinth's kitchen."

Nikki nodded and quickly pulled her wet, muddy boots back on.

They started down the steep pine-covered hillside, Griff in the lead. The pirate had put out her torch and the moon had gone behind a cloud. In the pitch blackness they stumbled and cursed and tripped on tangled tree roots. All of them were scratched and bashed by the time they reached the flat ground by the river. They were heading toward the road leading back to Clearwater Gardens when Griff suddenly whispered for them to halt.

Nikki quietly came up alongside Griff. The pirate was crouched down behind a blackberry bush. She pulled Nikki down beside her.

"Horse," she whispered into Nikki's ear.

Nikki peered into the darkness. She couldn't see anything, but over the rushing water of the nearby river she could just make out the quiet shuffle of hooves on dirt and the heavy breathing of a large animal.

Crawling on her hands and knees Griff inched around the blackberry bush toward a pile of boulders edging the road. Nikki followed.

When Nikki carefully peered over the top of the boulders a flash of silver caught her eye. The moon had re-appeared from behind the clouds and was shining on the armor of a man sitting on horseback. He was right in the middle of the road, as if standing guard duty.

Nikki and Griff watched the man for several long minutes, but he never budged from his post. A sword was belted to his waist and a long spear rested in a leather holder next to his saddle. Finally Griff signaled to Nikki and they crawled back to the others.

"Knight of the Iron Fist," Griff whispered in reply to Darius's quiet question. "We only saw one, but I'd bet an entire haul of codfish that there are more of 'em about. This bloke's smack in the middle of the road which leads from Clearwater Gardens to Friebergen. Just standing there as if he owns the right-of-way. My guess is he's got orders to prevent people from leaving Cogent Town."

"I thought the Knights of the Iron Fist had all gone back to Kingston," whispered Nikki.

Griff shrugged. "Looks like that little rat Rufius is handing out bribes again. Let's get back to the estate and under cover. We'll have to go along the riverbank. The road isn't safe anymore."

The trip back took them much longer than their trip up to the dam. There was no clear path along the river. Sometimes it was an easy walk along little bits of sandy beach edging the water, but most of the time they had to push and cut their way through tangled, pathless undergrowth. At times they even had to wade in the river.

Nikki breathed a sigh of relief when she finally spotted the turrets and gables of Lady Hyacinth's mansion. She had a deep scratch over one eye from shoving through a thicket of thorn bushes and her borrowed trousers were soaked from wading in the icy river.

Griff called a halt at the stone jetty which joined the estate's immense lawn to the riverside beach. They all crawled under an arch of the jetty and collapsed on the sand.

"Nip up to the rose garden and check on the rest of the crew," Griff said to one of the pirates. "See if they've spotted any Knights hanging around."

The pirate disappeared into the darkness.

Nikki tucked her hands inside her heavy wool sweater and tried to get comfortable on the sand. The stones of the jetty were too cold to lean against, so she curled into a ball and tried to drift off. She was sure the cold would keep her from sleeping, but before she knew it Griff was shaking her awake.

"Come on young codfish," whispered Griff. "It's not safe here. Our scout has returned with bad news. The place is surrounded by Knights. They're posted at every corner of the house and what's even worse they've rounded up my crew."

Nikki followed Griff as the pirate crept out from under the arch and alongside the jetty toward two small rowboats pulled up on the sand. Darius and the three pirates who'd been with them at the dam pushed the boats out into the river. Nikki climbed into one boat along with Griff and Darius, and the three pirates climbed into the other.

Darius took the oars and pulled strongly out into the main current of the river. He shipped the oars when the current took hold and they floated downriver toward Cogent Town. From her perch in the bow Nikki peered back at Lady Hyacinth's estate. The windows of the mansion were dark and she couldn't see any movement on the lawn. Trying not to think about the warm bed she'd slept in the night before, she determinedly turned her back on the estate and stared forward into the darkness.

"Keep a sharp eye out, young codfish," said Griff. "The river is navigable, but just barely. Lots of rocks and rapids in this area. I haven't been on the river for many years, but if I remember right it slows down and deepens just past the market square, near the warehouses and the smithies. We'll have to leave the boats there. There's a small dam across the water which powers a row of water-wheels. They're used by the tanneries to pound hides into leather. Boats can be portaged around the dam, but it makes more sense for us to leave the river at that point."

Nikki nodded and returned to watching the river. Griff wasn't kidding about the rocks. Nikki found herself frantically making hand signals to the left and right. Darius took up the oars again and pulled according to her directions. They managed to avoid capsizing, but there were many close calls and one loud crunch which knocked the left-hand oarlock clean off. Darius grabbed for the oar but it fell into the river and sank.

"Not to worry," said Griff. "We're getting close to the dam. The current will carry us the rest of the way."

The mansions and manicured lawns of Clearwater Gardens disappeared and the half-timbered roofs of Cogent Town began to line the riverbank. Griff took the remaining oar from Darius and used it as a rudder to steer the rowboat toward the left bank of the river. Loud voices from riverside taverns echoed over the water, but most of the other buildings were dark and quiet. The moon had set, making it impossible to see the pilings and small wooden piers which were jutting out into the river. They hit a piling with a loud crunch, nearly knocking Nikki overboard. Griff grabbed her by the sweater just in time.

"Climb," said Griff, pointing up the piling.

Nikki did her best, but it was an awkward business. The piling was coated with stinky, slippery tar and the handholds were few and far between. She had almost reached the top of the piling when she felt herself sliding back down. She dug the heels of her boots into the tar and somehow managed to scramble up the last few feet, dragging herself up onto the wooden platform by her elbows. A wooden barrel full of fishing rods, a pile of nets, and a bucket reeking of rotten fish proclaimed that this was someone's fishing pier. Nikki got to her feet and cautiously walked down the creaky pier while Griff, Darius, and the pirates struggled up the tar-covered pilings. Nikki reached the end and squinted at a small building facing the pier. It didn't look like someone's house, more like a fish-seller's shack. The door was closed and the windows dark.

"No food in there to steal," said a voice at her elbow. "I already checked."

Nikki whipped around. The blond hair of a little boy shone in the moonlight.

"Curio!" gasped Nikki.

"Oh my gosh, Miss! This is a lucky chance! Didn't realize it was you. I thought it was just some poor soul looking for a bite to eat."

"What are you doing here?" Nikki asked.

"Catching dinner," said Curio, holding up three trout hanging from a piece of fishing line. "I figured since these rods were so nice and handy I'd try my luck. Mr. Fuzz is out doing his usual borrowing, but I thought I should help out seeing as how we gots lots of mouths to feed."

"But," said Nikki, "surely the Prince will see to it that everyone gets dinner at his house. We're headed there now."

Curio shook his head. "Nope, Miss. We're all cutoff from the lap of luxury. After we noticed you was missing Mr. Fuzz, Miss Kira and Mr. Krill all went out looking for you. Mr. Bertie went out in his carriage to see if he could spot you around town anywhere. We didn't have any luck, but when we all tried to meet up again at the Prince's house we found it practically covered in knights. There was knights at the gate and knights in the front garden and even a couple seated on their horses and looking over the wall of the back yard. One of 'em spotted me but I climbed real quick-like over the neighbor's wall and hid in a lilac bush three houses down. Mr. Krill also got spotted, but he did a real fancy move where he jumped onto the roof of a passing carriage and lay flat. He rolled right by a bunch of knights on horseback and they never saw him. The Prince tried to help by distracting the knights after they spotted us, but he had to stay inside his mansion to look after his staff and Miss Athena, who can't walk yet. So now they're stuck there in the house. They can't get out and we can't get back in."

"That is unfortunate news," said Darius, joining them. "Where are you all staying? Has the King's nephew taken you in?"

Curio jumped a little, eyeing the stonemason warily. "No, sir," he said. "Mr. Bertie was staying with the Duchess of Falsa, and no way would she let rabble like us stay in her mansion. So Mr. Bertie decamped to his own place here in town. He's got fancy quarters up at the castle, but he figured his townhouse would be safer for us. Unfortunately, when Mr. Bertie arrived there he found that the knights had it surrounded. But they weren't real obnoxious with him, seeing as how he's the King's nephew. I hid up in a tree and watched them stop his carriage before they let him inside his own gates. It was pretty funny the way they danced around like nervous cats, despite all their armor and spears. They couldn't decide whether to be rough with him or to bow down to him. Anyways, he can get in and out of his house as he pleases, but him and Mr. Fuzz thought the rest of us should keep our distance. Mr. Bertie and Mr. Fuzz has been trading messages through the household servants when the servants go out on their errands. And Mr. Fuzz found us a hidey-hole. It's not a grand mansion, and the roof leaks, but it's better than being on the streets. I'll take you there. Let me just take care of these fish real quick."

Curio pulled a little knife out of his pocket and expertly gutted the fish, dumping the entrails in the river. He nodded to Griff and the pirates and motioned all of them to follow him.

At first he stuck close to the river, leading them past fishing shacks and churning waterwheels, but then he darted down a dark alley. It twisted and turned and was full of yowling alley cats fighting over scraps and fish heads, but eventually it led to the market where Gwen had found her pale-blue silk dress and pink satin cloak. The market was dark and deserted and all the stalls had canvas awnings pulled down over their wares. The narrow aisles between the stalls were muddy from a recent rain. Curio pulled open the tent-flap of a used-clothing stall and waved them all inside.

"Disguises," whispered Curio. "This is the best stall for 'em. I happens to know that the monasteries near Cogent Town send all their used cassocks here. The merchant pays good money for 'em cause the quality of the wool is top-notch. He pays a seamstress to rip 'em up and sew them into jackets for little boys. I used to have one me self. It was warm, but itchy as a coat made of bees. It gave me a rash on my arm shaped just like a duck. I used to hang out in the market here and charge people a penny to see it."

"Curio," said Griff, "Less chatter and more haste."

"Yes Miss Griff," said Curio. "They has 'em sorted by size. I think the biggest are over here."

Darius and the pirates followed him over to a trestle table piled high with dark cloth. They soon found cassocks which fit, along with deep hoods which obscured their faces. The long robes brushed the ground, hiding their boots. Griff was also able to find one which fit, but Nikki had less luck.

"That's not gonna work, Miss," said Curio, watching Nikki try to hold up her too-long cassock out of the dirt. "You look like a little girl playing dress-up in her Daddy's clothes. The Rounders'll spot you in a second. There ain't no smaller ones, as the monks don't allow women or children up in the monasteries. We'll have to find something else. Wait here. I has an idea."

Curio returned a few minutes later carrying a roll of linen bandages. "Wrap this around your hair and face, Miss. Lepers use these to hide their sores. Might make it a bit hard to see, but no one will recognize you. And monks sometimes care for the lepers and let them sleep in the stables of the monasteries, so no one'll think twice about seeing you following monks around."

Nikki wound the long linen strips around and around her head and tucked the ends into the neck of her wool sweater. She felt like a mummy in a horror movie, but she had to admit it was a good disguise. No one could possibly recognize her, and if they thought she had leprosy they'd likely keep their distance. She pulled at the strips until she had a narrow sliver to see through.

"Well, we all make a pious-looking set of monks," said Griff, pulling her hood down low over her face. "But what about you, young minnow?"

Curio responded by pulling his crumpled page hat out of this jacket and slapping it on his head. "If anyone stops us I'll do the talking. I'm a page from up at the castle and I'm leading you lot up to the King's private chapel. Lots of monks visit the chapel to pray and do other monk-stuff. Also the King gives 'em donations for their monasteries. That's a definite draw. Surprising how many monks are fond of money. Anyways, try not to speak. I better warn you that it's likely we'll get stopped and questioned. Lots and lots of roadblocks has suddenly appeared, starting two days ago. And a bunch of Knights of the Iron Fist suddenly arrived back in town. What with them and all the Rounders and the Lurkers it's a real headache to move around Cogent Town right now. Everyone pokes their nose into your business and wants to know who you are and where you're going. Anyway, line up single-file. Monks usually travel that way. And you, Miss, stay a little behind. Monks'll sometimes help lepers, but they ain't fond of getting too close to 'em. Can't say I blame them."

They filed out of the tent and Curio led them across the market square, walking quietly but not trying to hide. A few stray dogs growled at them, and a drunkard lurched at them asking for money, but they managed to walk quite a long way without anyone stopping them. It was only when they reached a part of the city consisting mainly of bakeries and other small shops that they encountered their first roadblock.

"Everybody quiet," hissed Curio, straightening his hat. "It's only Rounders. They ain't as sharp as the Lurkers or as dangerous as the Knights, but we still gotta be careful."

Nikki squinted through the strips of linen. A rough wooden barricade stretched across the street. Two men in Rounders uniforms were leaning against the barrier, arms folded. They had wooden clubs tied to their belts, but no swords or spears that she could see.

"Hi there chaps," said Curio cheerfully. "Lovely night ain't it?"

One of the Rounders snorted. He lazily strolled up to them, eyeing them up and down. "Bit early to be wandering around town. Only thieves and milkmaids are up this early. Where be you headed?"

"The Royal Chapel," said Curio, pointing to the tallest tower of Castle Cogent, whose flag was just beginning to glow purple in the first light of dawn. "You know how it is with monks. They likes to be up before the sun. I guess their prayers are more powerful if they're half asleep when they chants 'em."

The Rounder didn't reply. He walked up and down, trying to peer into the hoods of their cassocks. "What monastery did you say these here monks is from?"

"Well, I didn't say," said Curio. "But there's no harm in telling you that they've come all the way from the Trackless Forest. They walked all the way to Cogent Town on foot, just to see the glories of the castle and maybe catch a glimpse of the King."

"The King's busy nowadays," snapped the Rounder. "Too busy to make chitchat with wandering monks. And good luck getting that walking pile of bandages into the castle," he said, pointing at Nikki. "Rufius won't allow it. Quite the little neat-freak he is. I hear tell he takes four baths a day. My daughter's a washer woman up at the castle, and she says they're running out of soap up there. Little Rufius has to have a freshly-washed black tunic every two hours."

"Sounds like you're not a fan," said Curio.

The Rounder shrugged. "I is a fan of anyone who pays me. And little Rufius has doubled our pay. Hired new Rounders too. Said things was getting too slipshod and careless. Said Cogent Town needed to be ruled with a stronger hand. All new arrivals now has to present themselves to the Office For The Control of Strangers. It's down at the base of the castle, near the old vegetable market, next to the goose-seller's stall."

Curio nodded. "I knows it well. Us pages has to take all visitors there. Quite a pain it is, if you ask me. I had to take an important merchant from D-ville there yesterday, and oh my gosh did he kick up a fuss. They poked and prodded all his bags, and they were even insisting that he take off his clothes. Just his outer clothes, mind you. Cause no one wants to see a D-ville merchant in his underwear. Anyway, he slipped them a little gold and suddenly they lost all interest in searching him."

The Rounder chuckled. "A little gold is always helpful in these situations," he said, holding out his hand.

Curio flashed his most charming grin. "Don't I know it. But you see, yesterday I was guiding a rich merchant. Today it's just poor monks who've walked and walked . . ." He stopped suddenly. Griff had tapped him on the shoulder, two gold coins in her hand.

Nikki tensed. Even through her bandages she could see that Griff had a blue anchor tattooed on the back of her hand. It seemed an unlikely decoration for a monk.

The Rounder seemed to think so too. He stared at the tattoo, then bent and tried to peer under Griff's hood. Quick as a flash her hand disappeared back into her robe and appeared again holding two more gold coins. She dropped them into the Rounder's outstretched hand and motioned to Curio to proceed through the barrier.

Curio nodded and walked straight up to the wooden beam barring his way, as if he was going to walk right through it. At the last second one of the Rounders swung it open.

"Thanks Miss Griff," said Curio as they turned down a side street and were out of sight of the barrier. "That Rounder was a greedy one. If everybody has to pay four gold coins just to walk down the street then Cogent Town is gonna run out of money in a week." He sniffed the air. "Mmm. Smell that? Cinnamon sugar. Lovely smell. Means the bakeries are stoking their fires and baking their Cinnamon buns. I used to steal two of those a day when my master stayed here in town. Bruster's Bakery makes the best ones. They're dripping with glaze and big as a dinner plate." He jumped over a puddle. "We're just down here, behind the bakeries. Watch yer step. The wagons that deliver flour have been here and the horses have left gifts on the cobblestones."

Curio's warning came a bit too late. Darius swore as he stepped in a pile of horse manure so fresh that steam was coming off it.

"There's a horse trough here, Mr. Darius," said Curio. "You can clean off yer boots. Just nip down these here stairs when you're done." He quickly looked up and down the alley to see if they were alone then led the way down steep stone steps which dived under one of the bakeries.

Nikki wrinkled her nose under her bandages. The steps stunk of cat pee and mold.

Curio stopped at a door at the bottom of the stairs and knocked using a long, complicated pattern. The door swung open and Krill's tall frame loomed over him. Krill's leather tunic was torn and dirty and he held a knife at the ready, but he quickly sheathed it when he saw Curio. He hurriedly waved them inside.

"Hang on," said Curio as Krill was closing the door. "Mr. Darius is coming."

Krill snorted and muttered something that sounded like 'traitor', but he waited until Darius strode through the door before closing and locking it. He led them down a long hallway lined on one side with bricks.

The brick wall was oddly warm to the touch. Nikki was tempted to lean her whole body against it to soak in its warmth. A yeasty, sugary smell emanated from it and she guessed that on the other side wood-fired ovens were blazing away. The room Krill led them into seemed like an oven itself. It was lined with red bricks. Floor, walls, and ceiling. Sitting on crude wooden benches, sweat pouring down their faces, were Fuzz and Kira. They were watching a man kneeling on the floor. He was pouring out a line of black powder onto a piece of parchment.

"Sander?" asked Nikki in surprise. "What are you doing here?"

Sander looked up at her and nearly fell over, his eyes wide.

"Oh, right," said Nikki. "Hang on a second." She unwound the bandages from her head.

Sander let out a whoosh of relief. "Jeez, don't scare me like that. Can't stand lepers. Saw one in D-ville once. He was begging and when he held out his hand one of his fingers fell off."

"That was probably just Four-Fingered Jack," said Curio. "He's got a wax finger that looks just like a real one. He hangs out near D-ville City Hall and drops it to scare little kids. Sometimes he fills it with cherry jam so that it looks like its bleeding when he squeezes it."

"Stop the chitchat. Time is short," snapped Fuzz. "Glad you're back," he said to Nikki. "We'll need your help with this. Pour out the other one," he said to Sander.

Nikki took a seat next to Kira, who gave her a quick smile. They watched as Sander poured another line of black, sooty powder from a little clay jar. He got to his feet and looked at her expectantly.

"I'm guessing this is the powder that Geber mixed in his laboratory," said Nikki.

"This line over here is," said Sander, pointing. "It came from the pot he uses to fill his fireworks. This other line is from a pot I stole from his private chambers. It was in a secret compartment built into the wall under his bed. He thinks no one knows about the compartment, but I found it years ago."

Nikki nodded. The stolen pot was probably the one taken by the Lurker from Gwen's rooms in Deceptionville. She knelt down and scooped a bit of the powder into her palm. It was soft like talcum powder and smelled faintly of charcoal and sulfur. She pinched a bit of the other line between her fingers. It felt and smelled about the same, but she'd seen with her own eyes that Gwen's version was more powerful than the one Geber used for fireworks. Gwen had used it to blow a huge hole through the thick stone walls of the Southern Castle.

The original ingredients of gunpowder were charcoal, sulfur, and saltpeter, which was potassium nitrate. Nikki wondered what Gwen had added to make it more powerful. The saltpeter was an oxidizing agent. It added oxygen to the reaction and provided the explosive power. Maybe Gwen had discovered a new oxidizer. Nitrocellulose was one possibility. Nitrocellulose was an explosive propellant and it produced a more powerful explosion than the original black powder. It was created from wood or cotton pulp mixed with sulfuric and nitric acid, ingredients which were possible to obtain in the Realm and which didn't require modern technical equipment to create.

Though she wasn't sure about the nitric acid. She tried to think back to her last semester of chemistry. They had created nitric acid by adding sulfuric acid to sodium nitrate. The mixture was then heated and the nitric acid distilled. The process seemed well within Gwen's skills. But, if she remembered correctly, early versions of nitrocellulose were very unstable. It would spontaneously decompose, until European chemists developed stabilizers for it in the nineteenth century.

She looked dubiously down at the small mound of black powder lying in her palm. Had Gwen created an un-stabilized version of nitrocellulose, and was it about to explode in her hand? She carefully dribbled the powder back onto the parchment.

"What?" asked Fuzz, who was watching her closely.

"I think we should dispose of this powder," said Nikki. "Both powders. We definitely shouldn't store them here in this very hot room. Regular black powder, like the kind Geber created for his fireworks, is probably safe. It needs a fuse to ignite it. But this other powder might be unstable. It could explode at any time."

Sander scrambled to his feet and backed away to a corner of the room. The pirates, who'd been quietly standing against the wall, disappeared down the brick-lined hallway. Fuzz, Kira, Darius and Krill didn't move from their seats, but they all had a frozen look about them.

"How should we dispose of them?" asked Griff calmly. She'd been leaning against the wall, watching intently but not interfering.

"This powder," said Nikki, pointing to the line of fireworks powder. "It has an ingredient which is soluble in water. So dropping it into water will make it harmless."

Griff nodded. "I saw a bucket next to that horse trough outside," she said to one of the pirates hiding in the hallway. "Fill the bucket and bring it in here."

They all waited tensely until the pirate returned.

"Set it down here," said Nikki.

The pirate set the sloshing bucket down next to her and made a hurried retreat back down the hallway.

Nikki picked up the piece of parchment by its edges and carefully funneled the line of black powder into the bucket. The charcoal was harmless, and the saltpeter was soluble in water, but she found herself flinching anyway. She knew that alkali metals like sodium and potassium exploded violently when mixed with water, but sulfur did not. She'd known that since she was six years old, when her mother had brought tiny bits of various metals home from her laboratory, some in oil-filled glass jars. She'd put safety goggles on Nikki, pulled a bit of potassium out of its jar and tossed it into a puddle in their driveway. It had exploded in a shower of sparks which sent Bitsy, their neighbor's dog, darting under the nearest parked car. The piece of sodium had also exploded, but the yellowish sulfur had just sat there in the puddle, getting soggy.

"What about the other powder?" asked Fuzz. "Should we dump it in the water?"

"No," said Nikki. "I'm not sure what's in it." She turned to Sander. "Did you find any notes made by Geber about these powders?"

"Just a couple scraps of parchment," said Sander, pulling them out of his trouser pocket. "These was in the secret compartment with the pot o' powder."

Nikki took the scraps and unfolded them. The handwriting looked familiar. She guessed that it was Gwen's, though she wasn't sure.

"How come I can't read it?" asked Curio, looking over her shoulder. "I can read good even though I didn't go to school. Just taught myself from me master's books."

"It's written in code," said Nikki, squinting at the cramped writing. It wasn't the same code which she and Lady Hyacinth had deciphered. That code had used made-up symbols in place of letters. This used regular letters, but they were scrambled so that the text seemed like nonsense. Even worse, it was smudged and water-spotted in many places.

"Can you figure out what it says?" asked Fuzz.

Nikki shook her head. "No. I might be able to decode it, but it would take too long. It's encouraging that Sander didn't find any decoded pages in Geber's secret compartment. I think if Geber'd been able to decipher Gwen's code he would have written down the plaintext and hidden it in the compartment with the powder." She sat staring warily at the second line of powder. The best thing to do was to destroy both the powder and the coded notes so that no one could duplicate Gwen's work. The problem was how to safely dispose of the powder. If Gwen had added nitrocellulose to the powder then dropping it in water should be okay. Her memory about it was fuzzy, but she was pretty sure that nitrocellulose was stored in water. It only exploded when it was dry. She racked her brain, trying to think what other ingredients Gwen might have added to the powder. Nitroglycerin came to mind, but she couldn't remember what it was made of. Or if it was even possible to make it under the backward conditions in the Realm. She did remember that shaking it could cause it to explode. She wasn't sure about its reaction to water. More modern explosives like TNT required technical equipment and processes which weren't available in the Realm. The reality was that she just didn't know what was in the powder and she had no way of finding out. But it had to be destroyed. She carefully folded the parchment into a small packet around the powder and slowly stood up, the packet in her palm. "Open the door," she said quietly to Griff.

Griff nodded and strode to the door.

"Let me do it, Miss," said Curio.

"No," said Nikki. "Krill, keep him here."

Krill nodded and threw Curio over his shoulder.

"Then let me do it," said Fuzz.

"No," said Nikki. "The Realm needs you to lead the resistance to Rufius." She joined Griff, who was standing by the open door.

"Check that there's no one in the alley," said Nikki.

Griff disappeared briefly. "All clear," she said.

"Keep everyone in the room," said Nikki as she headed up the stairs to the alley.

She waited until she heard Griff close the door to the brick-lined room and then cautiously poked her head out from the stairway. There was no one in the alley except a mangy orange cat sunning itself on a windowsill at the far end. Nikki didn't give herself time to think. She took aim and tossed the small packet in a high arc. It seemed to float for a second in the air, then landed in the middle of the horse trough. Nikki dashed back down the stairs and crouched against the wall, her arms covering her head. She could hear a sizzling noise coming from the trough. She had no idea what it meant. It could be the prelude to an explosion, or it could just mean the water was deactivating the powder. She waited as long as she could, but she knew she couldn't stay there long. Someone might come down the alley and spot her. She climbed the stairs again and looked out. Smoke was rising from the horse trough, but no sparks. The orange cat had jumped down from its perch and was sniffing the smoke curiously.

"Well, whatever Gwen put in that powder seems to be deactivated with water," she said, rejoining the others in the brick room. "That's a useful bit of information."

"Do you think Gwen's made any more of the powder?" asked Fuzz.

Nikki shrugged. "I can't say for sure. This little bit that Sander found in Geber's chambers was probably the powder that Gwen demonstrated for us when we visited her in Deceptionville. We spotted a Lurker watching the demonstration, remember. He probably stole the powder from Gwen's room. And we know that Gwen used some of her powder to blow down a chunk of stone wall in the Southern Castle. That's how she escaped from its dungeon after

Rufius locked her in there. Whether Rufius has forced her to make anymore, I hope not, but I suppose she might do it if he threatened to kill her mother."

Fuzz nodded. "We should move Gwen's mother to a safe hiding place, just in case. As far as I know she's still staying here in town with the Duchess of Falsa."

"Gwen's mom is not very likely to cooperate," said Nikki. "I tried to talk to her after I left the Prince's mansion. She refused to believe that Gwen had valuable skills that made her a target for Rufius. And I couldn't even convince her that Gwen was missing."

"Yeah, Lady Ursula isn't known for her intellect," said Fuzz. "She has poodle-hair for brains. Maybe we can lure her out of the Falsa mansion, send Bertie's carriage for her or something."

Darius stood up. "I will go and collect Gwendolyn's mother," he said.

Fuzz snorted. "They'll never let you in. As the King's nephew Bertie stands a much better chance. He'll have no problem sweet-talking Lady Ursula into coming with him. I'll send a message by Bertie's kitchen maid. She'll be at our usual meeting place in three hours."

"No," said Darius. "That will take too long. I will go and retrieve Lady Ursula and bring her here. No sweet-talking will be required. I will just take her." He pulled his hood over his face and left the room without looking back.

"Well," said Fuzz, looking a bit startled. "I suppose that's one way to do it. Though if he's successful we're going to have an extremely upset Lady Ursula on our hands. And she's a handful even when she's happy."

"What are we going to do about Gwen herself?" asked Nikki. "We don't even know where she is."

"Bertie's working on that," said Fuzz. "He knows all the nobles in town, including the ones who've supported Rufius or taken bribes from him. His last message said he had a lead on where Gwen might be."

# Chapter Six

## The Count of Calumnia

WHILE THE OTHERS waited in their hideout near the town bakeries Curio slapped on his page hat and met Bertie's maid at their usual rendezvous site under a nearby bridge.

"Here you go, Mr. Fuzz," said Curio, returning to their hideout and handing Fuzz a scrap of parchment.

Fuzz stared down at it. "The Count of Calumnia," he said. "Well. That's a name I wasn't expecting. Bertie thinks he's the one holding Gwen."

"How weird," said Nikki, leaning against the warm wall of their brick-lined hiding place. "I just met him a few days ago. I waltzed with him at a party given by Lady Hyacinth at her estate. Tall guy, white hair, white goatee, very blue eyes. He said his name was the Count of Calumnia."

"Hmm," said Fuzz. "I wish I could talk to Athena. She has more contacts among the nobility than I do. I've always been more comfortable in taverns and on the streets than in ballrooms and parlors. Athena's the one with the parlor manners. The old girl has mentioned the Count to me once or twice, but not as someone to keep an eye on. As far as I know the Count of Calumnia is a strong supporter of the King. He's not someone I would've expected to join Rufius's takeover attempt." He pulled a piece of flint from his pocket, scratched it on a metal hook sticking out of the wall, and burned the scrap of parchment.

"You know Cogent Town better than I do," said Griff from a bench against the wall. "But from what I've heard the Count of Calumnia's mansion is practically a fortress."

Fuzz nodded. "Yeah, it's a bit of an oddball, architecture-wise. Most of the upper-crust mansions here in town are built for showing off and for staging fancy parties and balls. They have a lot of marble balconies and ballrooms and rose gardens, but not much in the way of defensive fortifications. But the Calumnia mansion was built over a thousand years ago, when there were endless civil wars in the Realm. Each noble family had their own armed troops and they were always fighting with each other. The Count's mansion has stone walls nearly as thick as those at the Southern Castle, and it's got its own moat as well. The moat's always been a bit of a problem for the town, as the Calumnia mansion is right next to the fish market. The fish sellers throw fish heads and other scraps into the moat. You can smell the stink from a block away."

"Are there tunnels underneath the mansion?" asked Nikki. "Maybe we can get in that way."

"A few," said Fuzz. "The Calumnia mansion is right at the base of castle hill and there are ancient tunnels all through that area. But it'll be much easier just to get invited in. That's where Bertie will come in handy. Nobody says no to a visit from the King's nephew." He ran his eyes over Griff, Krill, and the three pirates. "You lot will have to stay here. You're too threatening. What we need are small, non-threatening types. Maids, pages, stable boys." He pointed at Nikki, Curio, and Kira. "You three."

"Want me to nip back to the market?" asked Curio. "I can rustle up them type of costumes real quick."

"No," said Fuzz. "What we need are genuine King's Nephew uniforms. Bertie's official livery. Put your page hat back on and run over to Bertie's place. Say you have a message from the King. That'll get you in the front door. Then insist on seeing Bertie in person. Say it's a private message and the King requires a response. When you see Bertie tell him we need one parlor maid costume and two page uniforms. Bring them back here quick as you can. And tell Bertie to get himself invited to the Calumnia mansion."

Curio nodded and dashed out of the room.

Fuzz's normally cheerful expression suddenly turned serious. "I won't be able to go with you in this attempt to rescue Gwen," he said. "Imps have been fleeing Cogent Town in the last few weeks, and the ones who've stayed are harassed every time they set foot outside their houses. I'll attract far too much attention even in disguise." He fixed Nikki with a grim stare. "You'll have to lead."

Nikki felt a chill run down her spine despite the heat of the room. She was painfully aware of what Fuzz meant. The lives of Curio and Kira would be in her hands. She tried to shove down her rising fear and focus on a plan. "Do you think Curio has ever been inside the Count's mansion?" she asked.

Fuzz smiled faintly. "As far as I can tell that little pup has been just about everywhere in the Realm. But even if he hasn't I can describe the general layout of the place. I went there a few times with Athena, in better days."

Nikki nodded. "I assume you asked for a maid's costume because maids can go places in the house where a page can't."

"Yes," said Fuzz. "I thought it might give you more options. Kira can be the maid. You should stick with the page costume. The hat will help hide your face. Bertie's page uniforms have long green feathers hanging down one side of the hat. Bertie's very fond of feathers. He often wears hats with feathers that cover one eye, and his pages tend to imitate him. That'll take care of your face, but try not to talk. Let Curio do it if it's necessary. Did you talk to the Count at all when you were waltzing with him at Lady Hyacinth's?"

"A little," said Nikki. "But I was trying to disguise my voice. I don't think he'll recognize it. Also I had a veil over my face."

"All the same, try to avoid contact with him," said Fuzz. "He's a sharp old guy. Not easily fooled."

Kira stirred on her bench, her braids rustling. "Isn't it going to look odd if the King's nephew has a maid with him?"

"Nope," said Fuzz. "Bertie is notoriously fussy about his clothes and his hair. He frequently has a maid with him to spruce him up before a visit. I once even saw a maid powder his face during a card game. Startled the other players, let me tell you. Men in the Realm don't generally wear face powder. But none of the card players remarked on it. They're used to Bertie's eccentricities. Plus being a royal means he can get away with things that would get you or me laughed out of town." He picked up a twig from the floor and drew a rough circle in the dust. "The Count's mansion is basically a large, round stone tower. The outer walls are thick and crude looking, but the inside is very fancy, as you'd expect from such an old and noble family." He drew a spiral shape inside the circle. "It's got a strange layout. The hallways coil around and around an inner courtyard, with the floors going up at a slant. Rumor says that back in the civil war days the family guards used to ride horses up and down the halls. All the rooms are built against the outer walls, so they're all in a spiral too, one after the other until you reach the very top of the tower. At the top are guard rooms, arrow holes for archers to shoot through, and a row of cannons."

Nikki winced at the word cannons. Cannonballs could do serious damage, especially ones shot from the top of a tower located right in the center of the town. Even the weak version of black powder, the kind Geber used for his fireworks, could propel a cannonball a long distance if enough powder was used. About five hundred yards, if she remembered her medieval history correctly. "We should try to disable the cannons," she said.

"What?" asked Fuzz in surprise.

"The cannons," Nikki repeated. "Rescuing Gwen is our main goal, but if the Count of Calumnia is really in league with Rufius then we need to make sure they can't use those cannons. Cannonballs will go right through the wooden buildings which make up most of Cogent Town. They could destroy a huge area around the Calumnia mansion. Houses, shops, and people would all be smashed to pieces. It would be a terrible disaster."

"Speaking of disasters," said Griff from her bench. "I think it's time we told him about the dam."

"Clearwater dam?" asked Fuzz. "Yeah, I already know about that. Fortuna the Fortunate spilled the beans after we bribed her with a bag of gold. Rufius's plan is to destroy the dam using Gwen's more powerful version of black powder. To flood Cogent Town and create so much chaos and destruction that it'll be easy for him to depose the King and take power. But frankly I don't think it can be done. I've been up to Clearwater dam a few times over the years. It's unbelievably massive. The stones used to build it are as big as a house. I know Gwen used her powder to knock down a chunk of wall in the Southern Castle, but her powder would have to be ten times more powerful than that to take down Clearwater dam."

"Rufius doesn't have to blow up the whole dam," said Nikki. "Me and Griff have just come from the dam. We found the exact spot where they're planning on using Gwen's black powder. They left a mark in chalk. It's in an access tunnel on one side of the dam. There's a weak spot in the tunnel wall right there, near the spillway. Darius checked the tunnel wall and confirmed it. If they can blow up that part of the tunnel and open the spillway gates then the force of water rushing through will collapse the whole tunnel and very quickly eat away the hillside next to the dam. The entire reservoir will rush through and flood all of Cogent Town."

Fuzz just stared at her, a look of shock on his face. He opened his mouth to say something, but nothing came out.

"The only good news is that I don't think the flood would happen instantly," said Nikki. "It would take a day or two for the hillside to be worn away. We might have time to evacuate the town."

Fuzz shook his head. "There's no way we'll be able to convince the townspeople to evacuate. They might listen to the King, but I doubt we could convince him to give the order. He's always been good at going into denial about anything he doesn't want to believe."

"What about Mr. Bertie?" asked Kira. "He's on our side and he's the next best thing to the King himself. Surely the people will listen to him."

Fuzz stood up and started pacing. "Bertie's great to have on your side if you want to get invited to a card game at some nobleman's mansion, but the townspeople aren't going to listen to him about anything serious. People are polite to him because he's rich and royal, but they laugh at him behind his back. His face powder and fancy clothes and fussiness don't exactly inspire confidence in times of crisis."

"Well, then we'll just have to focus on getting Gwen back," said Nikki. "If we can't evacuate the town then we'll just have to make sure that no more of her powder gets made. I don't think they'll try their plan with Geber's fireworks powder. It isn't strong enough to damage Clearwater dam and I think Geber knew that."

"What baffles me is why they fixated on Gwen," said Fuzz. "What's to stop Geber from making a new version of his own powder? A stronger version."

Nikki shook her head. "Geber wasn't a good enough alchemist for that. I've seen Gwen's laboratory in the basement of Muddled Manor, and I've also seen Geber's labs in Deceptionville and up at Castle Cogent. Gwen's experiments and results are much more sophisticated. She's gone much farther than Geber in exploring chemical substances and how to combine them. A lot of Geber's stuff was trial and error, with a large heap of superstition mixed in. Also Geber's dead."

Fuzz's head jerked back. "Dead? How do you know?"

"I saw his body," said Nikki. "After I left the Prince's mansion I came across Geber shooting fireworks at imp houses. Trying to burn them down. He caused an explosion in an old flour mill which killed him."

Fuzz nodded, looking thoughtful. "That's good news. For us, anyway. But it's not quite as good as it sounds. Avaricious has been spotted here in town. Rufius will probably turn to him for alchemical expertise if he doesn't have Geber anymore. Avaricious is more of a merchant than an alchemist, but his shop in D-ville has dozens of experts in everything from metal smelting to face potions to acids. It's a good bet he's brought some of those experts with him."

"Do you know where he's staying in town?" asked Griff.

"No," said Fuzz.

Griff motioned to the three pirates, still in their monk cassocks. "Find out," she said. "And if you do find him you have my permission to smash any of his belongings. Particularly any bottles of powder or liquids."

"But don't dump them in the river," Nikki broke in suddenly, a picture flashing into her mind of the pirates dumping mercury, lead, or arsenic into the town's drinking water. "And if you do find powders or liquids be very careful with them. They could burn your skin or eyes."

The three pirates looked a bit unhappy at this news, but to their credit they just nodded, put up their hoods, and left the room.

"So everybody's got a job except me," said Krill grumpily from a far corner of the room. "What am I supposed to do? Just hang out here twiddling my thumbs?"

"Have a little patience," said Fuzz. "I might need you to take messages to the Prince of Physics. We're going to need his help before all this is over."

"I've got a job for him," said Griff. "The rest of my crew, over twenty men, were rounded up by the Knights of the Iron Fist. He could try to find out where they've been taken."

"I'll go right now," said Krill, practically leaping out of his corner.

"Slow down, Mr. Impatient," said Kira, frowning up at him. "He's always been like this. Ready for action without a thought in his head. One time when we were kids he jumped off a roof holding a bedsheet. He said the sheet would act like a kite and he'd land light as a feather. He didn't. He broke his ankle and two toes."

Krill just laughed and tugged at one of her braids. "Where should I start looking?" he asked Griff.

"The crew was camped on the grounds of Lady Hyacinth's estate," said Griff. "In Clearwater Gardens. If you follow the river north you can't miss it. Her estate is right on the river, with a huge lawn and a stone pier jutting out into the water above a small sandy beach. The men were in the rose garden. I left Jack Fuller in charge. I know you two haven't always gotten along, but I trust that if you find them you can put aside your differences and work together, instead of going at it like dueling swordfish. If you don't cooperate I'll throw both of you in the brig when we get back on our ship."

"They both like the same girl back in Kingston," Kira whispered to Nikki.

Krill ignored her and started for the door.

"Wait," said Fuzz. "You'll need a disguise. We'll have Curio find something for you."

Krill brushed this off with a wave of his hand. "Nobody knows me in this town. Even the knights who surrounded the Prince's mansion didn't get a good look at me. I was over the wall of the back garden and on top of a passing carriage in a flash."

"Some of the castle guards know you," said Nikki. "You spent days locked in a cell in their dungeon, remember."

Krill just shrugged. "The dungeon guards hardly ever leave Castle

Cogent. I doubt I'll run into any of them. And even if I do I'll just climb a wall and be long gone before they spot me."

"That's true," said Kira. "His head may be empty but his climbing skills are legend. He can climb from quarterdeck to crow's nest in the blink of an eye."

Krill grinned, gave them all a quick wave, and was gone.

Kira, Fuzz, and Griff stretched out on the benches to wait for Curio's return. Sounds of snoring soon echoed through the room.

Nikki knew she should try to get some rest. She hadn't slept much since her overnight stay at Lady Hyacinth's estate. But her mind was spinning in anxious circles, obsessing about their upcoming rescue attempt. She wished Griff was coming with them. It had been such a relief to follow the pirate's lead on their brief trip up to Clearwater dam. Being the one in charge was stressful. It was true that Bertie would be with them during their rescue attempt. As the only adult in their little group he should technically be the leader, but she knew why Fuzz hadn't told her to follow him. Bertie was nice enough, but he was the type of person who folded under pressure. She'd seen that in the Fox and Fig, when Bertie had faded into the background and left Darius to confront Rufius and his hangers-on. Unable to sleep, she gave up on getting some rest and began pacing up and down the room. She was on her one-hundredth lap when the door to the room suddenly creaked open. She peered down the brick-lined hall. It was Curio.

"Hello, Miss," he said, holding up a canvas sack. "Got them livery costumes Mr. Fuzz wanted. And a maid's dress for Miss Kira. Mr. Bertie also sent some nice pastries, with his compliments." He opened a paper sack and handed Nikki a gooey cinnamon roll.

"Hand over that sack," said Fuzz, sitting up with a yawn. He picked a scone out of it and handed the sack to Kira.

"Should we wake her?" Kira asked, nodding at Griff with her mouth full of cherry tart.

"Nah, let her sleep," said Fuzz. "We'll try to save her one, though I can't make any promises."

Curio sat down on a bench and dug into the sack with both hands, pulling out a raisin scone in his right and a lemon scone in his left. He took alternate bites, first from the left-hand and then from the right, scattering crumbs on the floor like a little blond buzz saw.

"So," said Fuzz. "How was Bertie?"

"Okay, I guess," said Curio, spewing crumbs. "He looked very nervous to see me, and he didn't say much. Just got me the livery and shoved me out the front door. There were a bunch of fancy gents playing cards in his parlor. I got the feeling that Mr. Bertie didn't want to be seen talking to a castle page."

"Hmm," said Fuzz. "Did you recognize any of them?"

"The Earl of Something was dealing the cards," said Curio. "You know, the one with the mustache that sticks out from his face like the horns on a bull. And the Duke of Mendacium was sitting across from him. The others I never seed before."

"I'm surprised at Bertie," said Fuzz. "I didn't think he had it in him."

"Didn't have what in him?" asked Griff, who was lying on a bench with her cassock hood covering her face. She sat up and waved at Kira to hand her the pastry sack.

"Courage," said Fuzz. "Mr. Mustache is the Earl of Barbarum. Possibly the nastiest piece of scum in the Realm. It's rumored that he's been responsible for quite a few murders over the years, though no one's ever been able to prove it. And the Duke of Mendacium isn't much better, though he tends to do more bribing than killing. They aren't the usual type that Bertie hangs around with. He must have invited them to a card game to try to get information out of them. I hope he's being careful. They're both capable of sticking a knife in his ribs. Being a royal won't save him."

"What about the invitation to the Count of Calumnia's tower?"

Nikki asked Curio.

Curio nodded, gulping down his last bite of raisin scone. "When Mr. Bertie was hustling me out the front door I asked him about getting into the Calumnia place. Don't worry, nobody heard us. We was already outside on the front stairs. Anyway, Mr. Bertie said he already had an appointment at the Count's mansion. He's going there for dinner tonight. He didn't say if it was a regular thing, or if he was doing more information hunting."

"Good," said Fuzz. "That settles it then. You three change into your livery and head over to Bertie's mansion. You should be able to walk openly through the streets. The Rounders aren't likely to bother the servants of a royal. Bertie will probably ride in his carriage over to the Count's place. Find a place to wait outside his gates, then try to flag down the carriage."

Nikki's eyebrows went up. "That seems a bit iffy. What if Bertie doesn't see us?"

"Then hop on while it's going," said Fuzz. "Bertie hates to drive fast, it gives him a stomach ache. He's got the slowest horses in the Realm. They rarely go faster than a walking pace." He opened the canvas sack and handed them their uniforms. He handed the empty sack to Kira. "Here, bring this with you. If the coachman asks why you're there just say that Bertie forgot his hat or his face powder or something. That should get you inside the carriage. The other two can ride on the back with the footman."

# Chapter Seven

## Card Games and Soapsuds

NIKKI TUGGED AT the collar of her forest-green page jacket as they slowly rattled along the cobblestone streets of Cogent Town. Her Westlake Debate Team T-shirt was sticking up out of her uniform. She wondered how the debate team was doing without her. Probably just fine, considering she'd lost her last match. At the Wisconsin State Championships, no less. She missed her teammates. Even Tina, the snarky team captain. And she missed her school, and her bedroom, and most of all she missed her mom.

She gave herself a shake. No time to dwell on all that. She needed to concentrate on the task at hand. She held on tighter to the iron bar she was grasping and leaned to one side to see around the back of Bertie's carriage. They were driving past the town's vegetable market. She spotted a stall selling geese. The frantic honking brought back memories of her first day in the Realm and she tried to spot the narrow alley where the portal back to her own world was. She recognized a water well decorated in bright yellow tiles. A woman in a worn cotton dress and canvas apron was heaving a bucket of water out of the well. Nikki smiled when she noticed that the woman was wearing mismatched woolen socks – one kelly green and one deep red. Some of the Realm's superstitions were still going strong. As far as she could remember the portal had been near the yellow-tiled well, and sure enough she soon caught a glimpse of the portal alley. The sun was setting and it was too dark to see far down the alley, but tears filled her eyes as she thought she recognized the spot on the wall where the portal had been. If the portal still worked then that spot would lead her back to the janitor's closet in her high school. She realized that her longing for home was growing stronger. It had never gone away entirely, but she'd been stuffing it down and focusing on the doings in the Realm. She'd be deeply sad if she never saw Fuzz, Athena, Curio, Gwen or Kira again, but she knew she didn't want to stay in the Realm forever.

She wiped her eyes as the carriage trundled past the vegetable stalls. The long steep road to Castle Cogent stretched up before them. Just when it looked like they were about to ascend to the castle they made a sharp left turn and rattled down a bumpy street at the base of the hill.

Fuzz hadn't been kidding about the fish smell, Nikki thought, her nose wrinkling. The stench was overpowering even though the fish market was nowhere in sight. A bit further on she finally spotted it, tucked away in a small square surrounded by gloomy stone buildings with shuttered windows. Most of the market stalls were closed for the day and only a few sad fish-heads remained, scattered across the ground and picked at by crows. A stone-lined moat curved around one corner of the square, its murky, smelly water lapping at the base of a hulking granite tower. Nikki tilted her head back to get a good look at the tower. It was as tall as a six-story building and very wide. She could just see the muzzle of a cannon poking out from the crenellations at the top. She wobbled as the carriage suddenly hit a pothole and nearly jolted her off. The footman standing beside her grabbed her roughly by the back of her jacket and hauled her upright.

"Thanks," she said, trying to sound like a teenage boy born and bred in the Realm. Through the green feathers dangling down from her page hat she could see the footman staring at her. Obviously her accent hadn't improved much. She turned away from him and peered around the carriage. They were approaching a stone bridge which arched over the moat. A guard in a purple cloak and chain mail stepped out from a wooden guard house and ordered the carriage to halt. The coachman called something to him. The guard nodded and stepped onto the running board of the carriage, peering inside. Bertie's high-pitched voice rang out, sounding irritated. The guard hurriedly jumped off, saluted and waved them across the bridge.

They rattled on across the bridge and under a dark stone archway cut into the side of the tower. Pieces of an old wooden portcullis which had rotted away stuck down from the roof of the arch like crooked teeth. The carriage emerged into a round courtyard which smelled of mold and horse manure. It was oddly empty. No flower gardens or fountains like the courtyards up at Castle Cogent. Not even any stacks of cannonballs or piles of firewood like those in the rough yards of the Southern Castle.

The carriage came to a halt and Nikki jumped off, wiggling her fingers. They were numb from hanging on to the iron bar for so long. Curio jumped off and stood quietly beside her while the footman opened the carriage door and helped Bertie and Kira out. Bertie was dressed in a long velvet coat of a startling acid-green color. His hat was a riot of blue, green, gold and scarlet parrot feathers. He reached into a pocket and handed Kira a tiny brush.

Fortunately Kira understood. She took the brush and carefully brushed Bertie's coat free of the dust of the journey.

Bertie inspected her work, brushed an imaginary speck of dust off his sleeve, fluffed up the feathers on his hat, and motioned them to follow him.

They followed Bertie in single-file, the footman first, then Nikki and Curio, with Kira last. Bertie led them to the only door in the courtyard. Its lintel was so low that Bertie and the footman had to stoop to enter. It led to a dark narrow tunnel whose walls dripped with water, as if the moat outside was trying to get in. At the end of the tunnel waited two more guards in purple cloaks, swords crossed in front of their chests.

Bertie waited while one of the guards knocked on a heavy oak door with the butt of his sword. The door creaked open on thick iron hinges. A gray-haired old man appeared in the doorway carrying a lighted torch which smelled strongly of pine sap.

"Good evening, your Highness," he said, the torchlight glinting off a row of embroidered silver fish decorating his sleeve. "The Count is in the card room, though I do not believe they have begun the game yet. The servants have built up a roaring fire, so you should be comfortable. The Count has requested that pork pies and ale be served during the game, but the kitchen staff will be happy to make something else if you would prefer."

"No, that will be fine, Montgomery," said Bertie, handing the old man his hat. "I'm here to play, not eat. I need to win back the money the Count took from me at our last meeting. Do you know who else is here?"

"The Earl of Barbarum, of course" said the old man. "He arrived just before your Highness. A few minor dignitaries from up at the castle are also here. No one you need to concern yourself with. I believe the Count invited them just to make sure there were enough players. And the King's advisor is here as well."

"The King's advisor?" asked Bertie, one of his hands twitching. "You surprise me Montgomery. I thought old Maleficious was dead and buried."

"And so he his, my lord. I was of course referring to the King's new advisor. Young master Rufius."

"Oh. Of course," said Bertie, clearing his throat nervously. "I'd forgotten about that young chap. I've only met him once. We chatted briefly at the Fox and Fig. Is he a good card player, do you think?"

"I couldn't say my lord," said Montgomery. "If you will follow

me." He led the way down a dark hallway which looked more like a
tunnel in a coal mine than a passageway in the house of a Count.
Water seeped down the rough stone walls and the floor was covered in
woven reeds instead of a plush carpet. Smoky torches shone dimly
from iron brackets bolted to the walls.

As they walked the floor started to slant and Nikki realized they
were walking uphill. It reminded her a bit of a wheelchair ramp. It
bent around in the spiral shape that Fuzz had described. They walked
quite a long way, going two full turns around the tower. The dripping
walls were a clue as to why the Count didn't live on the ground floor.
There was a line of mineral deposits well above Nikki's head,
obviously caused by water damage, and she guessed that the water in
the moat tended to flood in heavy rain and seep through the tower
walls. She supposed that the Count lived in the tower because it had
been in his family for so long, but personally she would have abandoned it for a small cozy house which didn't flood.

Montgomery halted next to a passageway which branched off the
spiral. A strong smell of yeast and baking bread poured out of it.

"Would you like your servants to wait in the kitchen, my lord?" he
asked Bertie.

Bertie gestured at the footman. "I'm sure he'll be very comfortable
there. The other three will accompany me."

Montgomery nodded and they continued up the spiral without the
footman.

Nikki saw Curio give her a look and she knew exactly what he was
thinking. It would have been easier to sneak away to search for Gwen
if they'd been left alone in the kitchen. She didn't have time to ponder
Bertie's motives however, as Montgomery had come to a halt next to
a huge oak-paneled door. With much straining and grunting he
swung it open.

The room they stepped into was a startling contrast to the dark,
damp spiral walkway. Its polished mahogany panels and gilt-framed

mirrors reflected the flames burning in a fireplace large enough to walk upright in. A rosewood card table dominated the center of the room and red velvet couches lined the walls.

Bertie motioned to Nikki, Curio, and Kira and they quickly took a seat on one of the couches farthest from the card table.

Nikki pulled at the long green feathers hanging from her page cap to be sure they hid her face. She'd spotted Rufius as soon as they entered. He was lounging in a velvet chair, his feet up on the card table. She hadn't seen him since ImpHaven, but he looked much the same as always, dressed in his usual spotless black tunic and leather sandals. His pale face had the beginnings of a beard, which made him look older than usual. He took a swig from a silver tankard of ale and watched with a slight smirk on his face as Bertie approached the table.

"Good evening, gentlemen," said Bertie, his voice quivering beneath its attempted heartiness. "Count, it's good of you to invite me."

"Of course," said the Count of Calumnia smoothly, rising from the table to shake Bertie's hand. The Count was wearing a sky-blue tunic embroidered with sliver thread which shone in the firelight. It gave his vivid blue eyes and white goatee an angelic quality which clashed with the fox-like cunning of his smile. "No doubt you are hoping for a reversal of our last meeting. I believe I was lucky enough to relieve you of an entire bag of gold."

A harsh laugh erupted from the other side of the table and a tall man with wild black hair and a dirty, stained tunic raised his tankard to Bertie. Two fingers on his right hand were missing, as were several of his teeth. He lifted a bag off the table and shook it, the coins inside rattling. "Let's see how quick you rodents are to take *my* gold," he said in a voice like sandpaper.

The Earl of Barbarum, thought Nikki. Curio was right, his mustache did stick out like the horns of a bull.

There were four other men at the card table, but they just politely nodded at Bertie and returned to sitting quietly, trying to avoid the attention of the Earl.

"Well, gentlemen," said the Count. "Shall we get started?'

Bertie nodded and took a seat at the table. The Count joined him and began dealing the cards with a quick, practiced hand.

For a long while there was no sound in the room but the crackling of the fire and the sound of coins clinking as they were thrown down in bets. The players barely looked up when a servant came in with a large silver tray piled with pork pies. The Earl of Barbarum grabbed two pies in one hand and grunted for another tankard of ale, but the others kept their eyes fixed on the cards.

Nikki noticed that Bertie wasn't drinking at all. And that the Count and Rufius were barely sipping from their tankards. It was obvious that they were hoping the Earl would get drunk and start making bad bets. It was unfortunate that they weren't all drinking heavily. If they all got drunk it would be relatively easy for her, Curio, and Kira to slip out of the room. As it was she felt pinned down by the glances Rufius kept throwing at them. She wasn't sure if he recognized her, or if he was just suspicious that they might somehow help Bertie cheat at cards.

More than an hour passed before the Count of Calumnia suddenly pushed his chair back from the table.

"Let's take a break, gentlemen," he said, pickup up a pork pie. "I need to clear my head before we begin another round." He went over to the fireplace to stand in front of its warm flames. Rufius and Bertie joined him. The Earl of Barbarum stayed at the table, devouring pork pies and occasionally throwing threatening glances at the other players. They studiously avoided his eye, which seemed to please him immensely. Every so often he'd flick a piece of pie crust at them. The crumbs bounced off their noses or stuck in their hair, but they didn't say a word.

"So, tell me Count," said Bertie, his voice trembling faintly, "why do you insist on staying in this damp old pile of rock? Surely there are much nicer places in Cogent Town you could purchase. I know of a lovely white marble mansion just down the street from my own which is up for sale. Wisteria vines in the garden, an arbor of grape vines surrounding an exquisite bronze statue of a stag. Its owners are moving to Kingston. I believe they have relatives there."

The Count of Calumnia shrugged. "I'm used to this old place. Plus its location near the castle is a useful reminder to the King and his courtiers that the family of Calumnia must be included in any doings of the Realm."

"And I believe your family charter requires you to live here," said Rufius, a smile playing on his lips. "Is that not so? Do you not have to relinquish your fortune if you leave this tower?"

The Count shot him an angry glance, his fingers tightening around his sliver tankard. "Yes, that is so, though I would very much like to know how you have learned this. It is private business known only to the Calumnia family. It is certainly no business of yours."

Rufius chuckled. "All doings in the Realm are my business," he said. "As the King's advisor I am his Majesty's eyes and ears. I would be remiss in my duties if I did not learn everything there is to know about the Realm's most prominent families."

"It must make quite a change from the doings of your own family," said the Count. "I believe they are cheese mongers? From some backwater town in the middle of nowhere. You've climbed quite high from your humble origins."

"They are from Popularnum," said Rufius, shooting the Count a murderous glance. "As you well know. And it's not where I come from but where I am now that matters."

"Quite so, quite so," said the Count smoothly. "But whether you will be able to stay in your current position is an open question. It would be wise to remember that your current position depends on the goodwill and support of those prominent families which you are so fond of investigating."

A smirk flashed across Rufius's face. "I have other sources of support."

The Count snorted. "Yes, those brainless thugs who ride around in armor and call themselves knights. They'll desert you as soon as the money runs dry." He threw a quick glance at Bertie, who had left the fireplace and was peering out of one of the narrow, rain-splattered windows. "And I'll tell you who else will desert you," he said in a voice barely above a whisper. "All those prominent families, if they discover that one of their own is currently being held in this tower against her will."

Nikki held her breath, straining to listen.

"I should never have agreed to be part of it," continued the Count. "A noble lady, locked in my dungeon like a common thief. The entire nobility will desert me if they find out. I'll be forced to leave the Realm. I'll have to live out my days in some ghastly northern kingdom, with yokels for neighbors and pigs rooting in the streets."

Rufius shrugged. "Well then I suggest you make sure they never find out. And by the way, there are now two noble ladies locked in your dungeon, not one. While you were drinking glowworm in the Fox and Fig I collected the lady's mother and brought her here."

Nikki stifled a gasp. Gwen's mother, Lady Ursula, was here in the tower. Darius had failed in his attempt to get her to safety. That was not good news. Gwen, if they could get to her, would be a great asset in her own rescue. But Lady Ursula was going to be nothing but a burden. A noisy, complaining burden.

"Lady Ursula!" gasped the Count, turning as pale as his white goatee. "She's my second cousin on my mother's side! My entire family will rise against me! I only agreed to let you bring Gwendolyn here because she is extremely unpopular among the nobility due to her odd life choices. Messing about with chemicals and working in a shop in Deceptionville, of all things! But Lady Ursula, despite her rather annoying personality, is a pillar in the noble community. This will ruin me!"

"Keep your voice down!" snapped Rufius. He darted a glance at Bertie, who was still studiously examining the raindrops on the window panes. "And keep your head. You won't come to ruin if you remain calm and do as I say. Now, let's rejoin your guests and resume the card game."

They sat back down at the card table and Bertie joined them. The Earl of Barbarum had worked his way through several more tankards of ale and was now singing at the top of his voice as he dealt the cards. His aim was poor and many of the cards flew off the table and landed face-up on the floor.

"Earl, old chap," said Bertie, retrieving the fallen cards. "Why don't you let me deal this hand? I don't believe the Count and his guests are familiar with this style of play."

"No!" roared the Earl, banging his tankard down on the table. "And don't touch those cards, you rotten pig of a cheater! I saw you slip one in your pocket and another up your sleeve."

"I never . . ." was all Bertie had time to say before he was forced to jump up from his chair as the Earl threw his tankard at him and overturned the heavy rosewood card table as if it was made of paper. The other players scrambled away as cards and gold coins flew everywhere.

The Count ran to a velvet rope hanging near the fireplace and gave it three urgent pulls. A bell tinkled somewhere outside the card room and seconds later servants and guards rushed in. The Count gestured at the Earl of Barbarum, who was beating one of the card players with his silver tankard. Blood spurted from his victim's nose as Bertie stood helplessly by, looking guilty for not interfering.

Rufius retreated to the fireplace, a smirk on his face, clearly enjoying the show.

Despite being vastly outnumbered, the Earl took a long time to subdue. By the time the Count's guards pinned him to the floor two windows had been smashed and all of the card players were nursing injuries except for Bertie, Rufius, and the Count, who had all carefully stayed away from the skirmish.

The guards were dragging the Earl of Barbarum to the door when he suddenly roared loud enough to shake the broken windows and wrestled himself free. He made a run for Rufius, who dived behind the upturned card table.

Nikki saw her chance. "Now!" she whispered to Curio and Kira. They scrambled off the velvet sofa and sprinted toward the open door. One of the servants made a half-hearted attempt to block them but Nikki dodged around him and the others followed. Kira paused uncertainly in the hallway. Curio turned to go up the spiral.

"No!" said Nikki. "Down, not up. We need to find Gwen, and the Count said she was in the dungeon."

"But Miss," said Curio. "There's a cart full of firewood just up here." He frantically began throwing logs off of a wheeled cart which was parked against the wall near the card room.

Nikki and Kira both caught on at the same time. They ran to the cart and threw the remaining logs off. Curio kicked a chock of wood out from under the front wheels of the cart and jumped on. It started rolling down the slanted hallway. Nikki and Kira jumped on as the cart picked up speed, the sound of its wheels rattling along the coal-black walls. Curio grabbed the handle of the cart and tried to steer, but by the time they reached the first bend in the spiral the cart was going so fast Nikki was afraid they were going to tip over.

Curio steered the cart wildly from side to side in an attempt to slow down. Its metal wheels scraped against the rocky walls and threw up bright red sparks. At the next bend the cart tilted up on two wheels. Nikki and Kira threw themselves to the side and the cart slammed back down, nearly throwing Curio off. Nikki grabbed him by the back of his page jacket just in time.

Somehow they managed to careen around three more turns of the spiral without crashing, though Kira had bloody knuckles from a close scrape against the wall. They raced past a startled servant carrying a basket of laundry on her head, and then by another with a pile of sheets in her arms. The air became thick with the smell of soap.

They must be near a laundry room, thought Nikki as she threw her weight to the other side of the cart. It made sense that the laundry room would be down by the moat where there was a source of water.

"I think we're slowing down, Miss," said Curio.

"I think you're right," said Nikki. "The floor isn't slanting as much. Can you stop? We'll look less suspicious on foot."

"This thing ain't got no brakes, Miss," said Curio.

"Okay," said Nikki. "We'll wait for it to slow a bit more, then jump."

The smell of soap was becoming much stronger, and slimy streaks of it appeared on the walls and floor. Curio had just steered into a curve when their cart hit a patch of soap on the floor and spun wildly out of control.

"Sheets, Miss!" shouted Curio.

Nikki didn't have time to ask what he meant. Curio yanked hard on the cart's handle and they all went head over heels. As she flew through the air Nikki braced for impact with the hard stone floor, but to her surprise what she landed on was wet, soft, and squishy. Beside her she heard Kira laughing.

"Sheets," said Kira, holding up a wet, white lump. "These must be all the sheets from every bedroom in the tower, judging by the size of this pile."

"Not a bad landing, if I do say so meself," said Curio, retrieving his page hat from the floor and clamping it back on his head.

Nikki scrambled out of the pile of sheets and adjusted her own hat so that the soggy and soapy feathers hid her face.

"Hey! What're you miscreants doing down here?"

They whirled around. A fat, red-faced woman in a rough dress and soapy apron was waving a scrub brush at them.

"Um . . .," said Nikki.

"This ain't no place for strange servants to be messing about," said the woman. "Only the Count's laundresses is allowed down here. Who do you belong to, anyway?"

"We serve in the house of the King's nephew," Kira said quickly, curtseying to the woman. "Our master tasked us with acquiring new sheets for his bed. He is not satisfied with the ones he has been provided with. They are not soft enough. We are to bring him a variety of sheets so that he may choose the ones he likes best. And your best goose-down quilts as well."

The woman's mouth dropped open, but no sound came out.

"Not to rush you, ma'am," said Curio with a little bow, "but our master's card game is nearly over and he wishes to retire to bed directly after."

"Right," said the woman, still looking at little dazed. "Well, come this way. My goodness. It's not every day that our bed linens are slept on by the King's nephew. I don't recall his Highness ever staying here before. Don't he have his own place here in town? I seem to recall him having quarters in the castle itself, and a grand mansion as well."

"He does, ma'am," said Kira. "But the Count was good enough to offer him a bed for tonight, as he has a slight stomach ache and the carriage ride home will make it worse."

The laundress nodded. "I've told our cook time and time again that her food is too rich. She stuffs cream and butter into everything, as if she's trying to fatten our guests like pigs to the slaughter. It's no surprise to me that some of 'em get a dodgy stomach." She led them under a low arch which cut through the stone wall and opened into a vast, steamy room. "Watch yer footing in here. Very slippery. Stay on the mats."

They followed her along a path of wet, soapy straw mats which wound through the room. Huge iron vats of boiling water hung from chains bolted to the ceiling. Servants rushed around throwing logs onto fires beneath the vats, while others stood on stools and stirred the laundry which bubbled away.

"These are the clean ones," said the laundress, leading them into a side room lined with wooden shelves piled high with folded sheets, blankets, and tablecloths. "There are some nice linen sheets with lace trim, or if his Highness prefers we also have some silk ones. Them ain't too popular, as guests tend to slide off them. We had an elderly countess slide right off the bed once. Broke her arm, the poor old dear. Never stayed here again."

Kira rubbed the corner of a sheet between her fingertips. "There are very nice, but his Highness has asked for a large selection to choose from. Please don't let us keep you, ma'am. I will choose a variety of sheets and a few blankets as well. These pages can help me carry them."

"All right dearie," said the laundress. "It's me break time anyway. Looking forward to a nice cup of tea and a hot bun with loads of butter. Give me regards to his Highness."

Curio poked his head out of the door. "She's gone," he said. "And no one else seems to be paying us any mind."

Nikki nodded. "Let's load up on sheets. We'll use the same story if anyone else asks us why we're down here. It's a lucky thing Kira is such a good liar." She and Kira loaded themselves up with linen sheets and pillowcases while Curio grabbed a goose-down comforter so puffy he couldn't see over it.

When they left the linen room they got a few glances from the workers tending to the laundry vats, but no one stopped them. As she walked past the vats Nikki noticed that the water to fill them came from iron pipes laid out along the stone floor. All the pipes converged into one large pipe which went straight through the outer wall. The room must be below water level, Nikki thought. If it wasn't then there had to be some kind of pump to pull water up from the moat into the room. An Archimedes screw would work. She'd seen that kind of simple pump in the Realm before. It was basically just a wooden or metal helix wrapped around a central core which pulled water up the turns of the screw. But it needed a source of power. In the Realm that was usually a water wheel or a windmill. But she hadn't seen either of these attached to the tower on the outside. She filed the pipes away in her memory as possibly useful in escaping from the tower. Maybe she and Gwen could come up with a way to use the steam power generated by the boiling vats of laundry. They were going to need an escape plan, because if they managed to rescue Gwen and Lady Ursula they couldn't just waltz out the front door of the tower with them.

"Now what, Miss?" whispered Curio from behind his puffy comforter. They'd reached the outer hallway without any interference from the laundry workers.

"Keep going down," said Nikki. "We must be near the dungeon. If anyone stops us we'll just say we're lost."

They gingerly walked along the slanted hallway, their feet sliding in the stream of soap bubbles which burbled out of the laundry room door and flowed downhill. Curio hit an especially slippery patch and slid down like a skier on a slalom course until he finally crashed face first onto his puffy comforter.

"Now I thinks I know why we ain't seen no guards down here," he said as he re-folded his soggy blanket. "With those metal-shod boots they wear they'd slip and break their necks in no time. The Count'd have to spend half his family fortune just to replace his guards every year."

"But there's sure to be at least a few guards watching the dungeon," said Kira. "What are we going to do when we meet one?"

"I'm not sure," said Nikki.

"Well, Miss," said Curio. "You'd better come up with something fast." He pointed down the hallway.

Their way was blocked by a metal grate that ran from floor to ceiling. In front of it sat a guard asleep on a wooden stool, a tankard of ale and a plate of chicken bones at his feet.

"Do ya think we can slip by him, quiet-like?" whispered Curio.

"I doubt it," whispered Nikki. "Even if we could we still need the keys." She pointed at a door in the middle of the grate. It was locked with a large padlock.

"Leave it to me, Miss," whispered Curio. He set down his comforter and slowly crept toward the sleeping guard. When he was a foot away Curio stopped and bent down, taking a long look at the guard. He seemed to find what he was looking for. His hand inched into the front pocket of the guard's tunic and slowly withdrew an iron ring. A mass of heavy keys hung from it. Curio grasped the keys to keep them from clanging and tiptoed to the door.

Nikki and Kira joined him. The first key he tried didn't fit. As Curio was trying the next key the guard suddenly snorted. Nikki whirled around, wondering if the three of them could overpower him. But he just shifted on his stool and began snoring.

"Try the biggest ones," whispered Nikki. "This is probably the main gate. The smaller keys are probably for prison cells."

Curio tried the other large keys with a shaking hand. Finally the lock clicked open. He was about to push open the door when Nikki laid a hand on his arm. She scooped up a handful of soap from the floor and rubbed it into the hinges of the door. When she pushed at the door it swung open soundlessly. Curio tucked the keyring into his page tunic and retrieved the soapy comforter.

Kira closed the door softly behind them and they headed down into the depths of the dungeon, the guard's snores fading away.

# Chapter Eight

Steam Power

"THIS DUNGEON SEEMS like it ain't never gonna end," said Curio. "Don't know why they had to dig it so deep. Ain't no prisoners down here far as I can tell." He ran a finger along the pitch-black wall. "Don't this seem like coal to you, Miss? There's coal mines north of Cogent Town."

Nikki ran a finger along the same patch and held it under the light from one of the smoky torches bolted to the wall. Her finger shone with a greasy, rainbow sheen, like an oil patch on a hot parking lot. It smelled faintly like rotten eggs, which indicated sulfur. "It might be bituminous coal," she said. "I wonder if these tunnels link up to the coal mines. Maybe we could get out that way."

"Maybe, Miss," said Curio doubtfully. "But it's an awful long way, even if they do connect up. My guess is we'd have a heap of trouble getting old Lady Ursula to walk that far. And she'd be complaining at the top of her lungs the whole way."

"Yes," sighed Nikki. "Gwen's mother is going to be trouble."

"Shush!" hissed Kira. "I hear voices."

They froze, peering down the tunnel. The sound of two female voices arguing was just barely audible over the crackling of the torches.

Nikki waved them forward. As they rounded a bend in the tunnel small slits in the walls appeared, light shining out of them. The voices grew louder. Nikki stopped and put her ear to one of the slits. One of the voices was Lady Ursula's high-pitched whine.

"Gwendolyn!" snapped Lady Ursula. "You aren't listening to me!"

"I'm listening, mother," came Gwen's voice, hoarse and tired. "But it isn't helpful to keep repeating the same thing over and over again. I'm not going to make any more black powder and that's final."

"But you must!" said Lady Ursula. "I insist! I am your mother and you must obey me. It's simply unbelievable that my own daughter refuses to get me out of this filthy dungeon. Not when she has the means to do so right at her fingertips. How can you stand there and tell me that it's impossible?"

"It's not impossible," said Gwen. "It's immoral. Those are two entirely different things."

Lady Ursula sniffed loudly. "How can you play word games when I'm sitting here on cold iron with my bones turning to ice? I haven't eaten since yesterday. Do you want me to starve to death?"

Gwen sighed. "You won't starve to death in one day, mother."

Nikki turned to Curio and Kira. "Gwen and her mother are right on the other side of this wall," she whispered.

"Well come on then," whispered Curio. "I got the keys."

"What if there are more guards?" whispered Kira. "Not every guard in this place is going to be asleep."

Curio gave an impatient snort and started down the tunnel, but Nikki grabbed his arm.

"Kira's right," she said. "The three of us don't stand a chance against even *one* guard. Not if he's awake. You two stay here."

Nikki crept back to the slit on the wall and tried to peer through. She caught a brief glimpse of flickering firelight, but that was all. Standing on her tiptoes she put her mouth to the slit and hissed.

"Gwen!"

The two quarreling voices suddenly ceased.

"Gwen!" Nikki hissed again. "It's me. Curio and Kira are here too. We're going to get you out."

"Nikki?" whispered Gwen through the slit.

"Yes," said Nikki. "It's me. Do you know how many guards are down here?"

"There aren't any here in the cell with us, thank goodness," said Gwen. "But there's one right outside the cell door. He peers in at us sometimes, through a barred window in the door."

"Is he armed?" asked Nikki.

"Yes," said Gwen. "He has a sword belted to his waist."

"Oh boy," said Nikki. "The three of us against a man armed with a sword. Those are not great odds."

Gwen was silent for a moment. "I have an idea which I think will work," she finally said. "Get as close to the guard as you can without being seen. He's just around the corner from you. Be ready to grab his sword. I think I can make something which will disable him. It will take me a while to prepare it."

"Okay," said Nikki. "We'll be ready." She turned to Curio and Kira, a finger to her lips.

The three of them crept silently along the tunnel, hugging the wall. Nikki was in the lead, and when she spotted a booted foot stretched across the floor she signaled to the others to halt. It looked like the guard was sitting with his back to the tunnel wall. A faint sound vibrated along the walls. The guard was humming to himself. Across from him Nikki could see part of the cell door and the barred window Gwen had mentioned.

They waited for what seemed like hours, barely moving a muscle. Nikki fought against her body, which insisted she needed to scratch, cough, and sneeze. Her legs were beginning to cramp up when she finally heard Gwen's voice and saw a flash of movement behind the barred window.

"Food!" Gwen shouted through the bars. "We need food! We haven't eaten in more than a day and my mother is faint with hunger."

The guard slowly got to his feet and sauntered to the door. "You'll get fed when you've done what they want. Not before. Rufius says you've had it too easy. He wants you to hurry things along."

"But my mother is ill," said Gwen. "Come, look at her. She can barely stand on her feet."

The guard snorted, but put his face to the window. There was a splashing sound and the guard yelled and staggered back, wiping at his eyes. He made a hoarse, choking sound and suddenly collapsed on the stone floor of the tunnel.

Nikki ran forward and pulled his sword from its sheath. She stood over him as Curio and Kira rolled him over.

"He's out like a light, Miss," said Curio, pulling up one of the guard's eyelids.

Nikki nodded. "Open the door," she said.

Curio pulled out his massive ring of keys and started trying them one by one.

"Hold them up so I can see them," said Gwen through the bars.

Curio held up the keyring.

"Most of those are room keys," said Gwen. "They're a common key design used in very old homes. I used to have a key just like those, for my childhood bedroom in Muddled Manor. Try that thick one that looks like an iron fork. It seems more like a dungeon key."

Curio nodded. He stuck the key in the lock and turned it. A loud clank reverberated through the tunnel and the heavy iron door of the cell swung open.

Gwen rushed out and knelt by the guard, feeling the pulse in his neck. She was still wearing the blue silk dress she'd worn to the Fox and Fig tavern. The bright color was a startling contrast to the coal-black tunnel.

"He'll be okay," Gwen said, relief in her voice. "It's a tricky mixture. Too much sulfuric acid and you'll cause terrible burns. And even if the mixture is correct, if the person inhales too much of the liquid it can cause paralysis of the lungs and then death."

"What was it?" asked Nikki, looking down at the guard. His face was an unhealthy shade of red, but otherwise he looked unharmed.

"It's called Oil of Peace," said Gwen. "Healers in the Realm sometimes use it when they have to amputate a leg or arm. It causes unconsciousness, but as I said it's very tricky to use, so most healers prefer to stick with getting the patient drunk. It's a combination of sulfuric acid and ethyl alcohol, which are heated and then distilled. But you have to get the ingredients in exactly the right ratios. Fortunately I had the components in our cell. From what I can tell Rufius sent someone to Muddled Manor and they brought the entire contents of my old laboratory here to the Count of Calumnia's tower."

Sulfuric acid and ethyl alcohol, thought Nikki. In her world it was called diethyl ether and it had been discovered around 1500. It had been used for centuries as a general anesthetic, but it was extremely flammable and wasn't used for surgery anymore.

"Help me get him into the cell," said Gwen, putting her hands under the guard's shoulders.

Nikki and Kira each took a leg and the three of them awkwardly trundled the guard through the cell door.

"Over here," said Gwen. "Under this workbench."

They shoved the guard back into the shadows and pushed some large clay pots in front of him. Gwen took a quick look out into the tunnel and then shut the cell door.

"The guards don't change shifts until midnight," she said. "We should have a few hours." She quickly gave each of them a hug and then sat down on a tall stool in front of a workbench piled high with pots, mortars, and glass jars. Red-hot coals glowed in a brick fireplace at the back of the cell.

Nikki, Curio, and Kira took a seat on an iron cot bolted to the wall. Lady Ursula paced in front of them dressed in a gray satin ball gown and a coal-smudged lace shawl. She raised her eyes to the ceiling and sighed loudly.

"These are our rescuers?" she exclaimed. "They're children! I suppose this was planned by those two blasted imps who are always hanging around the King. It smacks of their incompetence. They might as well have sent my poodle. At least he can bite."

"Be quiet, mother," said Gwen. "Now, what is your plan?"

"Um," said Nikki. "Well, to be honest we don't really have one. We're lucky to have gotten this far."

"Humph!" exclaimed Lady Ursula.

"Mr. Bertie is upstairs," chimed in Curio.

"The King's nephew?" asked Lady Ursula, halting her pacing.

Curio nodded.

"Well!" exclaimed Lady Ursula. "That is much better news! No one would dare refuse royalty. He will be able to get us out of here in an instant. We have only to wait here patiently until he comes down."

Nikki and Gwen exchanged glances.

"Rufius has gained tremendous control over the King himself," said Gwen. "I very much doubt he'll follow orders from the King's nephew."

"Nonsense!" said Lady Ursula. "That young gentleman Rufius is an ardent admirer of mine. He was gracious enough to pay us a visit at Muddled Manor, remember. He was profuse in his praise of my rose garden. And I've known Bertie since he was a baby. I'm sure I can convince the two of them to work out their differences and release us from this horrid place. And besides, I'm sure it was that worthless Count of Calumnia who ordered us thrown into this dungeon, not young Rufius. You'll see. Bertie and young Rufius will be down here in short order and I'll throw myself on their mercy. They won't be able to resist the entreaties of a noblewoman."

Gwen's face twisted into an odd expression halfway between an eye-roll and a smile. "Well," she said, "just in case that doesn't work out, let's mull over some alternate ideas."

"We was considering the coal mines, Miss," said Curio. "Now, I ain't never been in this tower, but I was guessing these tunnels might link up to the mines." He shot a sideways glance at Lady Ursula. "Problem is, it'll be a powerful long walk. All the way under Cogent Town to get to the nearest mines north of town."

Gwen shook her head. "I've seen maps of the mines you're talking about. Avaricious had maps of all the mines in the Realm. When I worked in his shop in D-ville I used to study his maps when I needed mercury, or arsenic, or other ingredients for my potions. The coal mines near Cogent Town don't go under the city. The coal seams stretch eastward."

"Maybe we don't have to go that far," said Kira. "Fuzz mentioned that this whole area of the city is crisscrossed with old tunnels. We're right next to Castle Hill. We might be able to find a tunnel which leads up to the castle. We could throw ourselves on the mercy of the King."

Gwen nodded thoughtfully. "Maybe," she said. "The King knows me, and he knows mother. It's unlikely he would just hand us over to Rufius, despite the control that little rat has over him."

"That's not a bad plan," said Nikki. "But there's no guarantee we'll be able to make it to the castle. The tunnels in this dungeon might come to a dead end and then we'd be trapped. Also there's the Mystic men to consider. It's a long story, but the short version is that they're a large group of men from the Mystic Mountains who are hanging around Castle Cogent. And they tend to be violent. Me and Curio were posing as pages up at the castle and saw them come bursting right into the throne room. Rufius has had dealings with them. They may even take orders from him. And I think they'd have no problem attacking the King himself. So expecting the King to keep us safe is not exactly a foolproof idea. I say we leave the tunnels as Plan B. I have a different idea which might work. It involves the laundry room. If it works it'll be a quicker way to escape than the tunnels. But it might be dangerous."

At the word 'dangerous' Lady Ursula plopped down onto the end of the iron cot and folded her arms. "I am *not* going to be subjected to any hare-brained schemes dreamt up by a child. I will wait here until Bertie arranges my release."

"You can't stay here, mother," said Gwen. "They'll just use you as a pawn. Even if I do manage to escape they'll threaten to kill you if I don't return and make the black powder they want."

Lady Ursula just harrumphed.

"What about just walking out the front door of the tower?" asked Kira. "We're still in our servant's uniforms. They've worked pretty well so far. We just need to find disguises for Gwen and Lady Ursula."

Lady Ursula looked at her as if Kira had suggested she eat a bowl of worms. "I will *not* under any circumstances dress up as a *servant*! The very idea! Our family has been among the highest ranks of the nobility since before Castle Cogent was even built. Our family is older than the family of the King himself."

Curio gave her a sideways glance, then leaned over and whispered in Nikki's ear. "Laundry basket."

Nikki looked at him in confusion.

Curio pointed at Lady Ursula, mimed throwing something at his own face, and then closed his eyes and faked a snore.

"Oh," said Nikki. She stood up and went over to Gwen. Their whispered conversation first left Gwen looking horrified, then thoughtful, then finally unhappy but resolved.

Gwen got down from her stool, ripped off a piece from one of the sheets Kira was still carrying, dipped the sheet into a stone bowl on her workbench, and approached her mother.

Lady Ursula was staring petulantly at the floor, not paying Gwen any attention. Before she realized what was happening Gwen had pressed the wet cloth over her nose and mouth. The instant Lady Ursula's eyes started to close Gwen removed the cloth. She quickly checked her mother's pulse and listened to her breathing.

"She's okay," Gwen said with a shaking voice, laying her mother down on the iron cot. "She'll probably have a headache when she wakes, but otherwise she'll be alright."

"How long will she be asleep?" asked Nikki.

"It's hard to say," said Gwen. "An hour, maybe two."

Nikki nodded. "That should give us enough time." She thought for a moment. "It was getting dark when we arrived at the tower, and I'd estimate we've been here about three hours. It must be past 8pm. The laundry workers should be done for the day and the laundry room deserted. Fortunately you two seem to be the only prisoners in this dungeon, and we've only encountered two guards. Our first obstacle will be getting past the guard who was asleep at the dungeon's main gate."

Gwen nodded. "You bring the sword and I'll bring a bottle of Oil of Peace."

"And I'll bring this, Miss," said Curio, holding up the soapy comforter he was still carrying. "Maybe we can throw it at him and wrap him up before he knows what's what."

Kira jumped off the iron cot and pulled a coil of rope out from under the workbench. She made a loop at one end and whirled the rope over her head. When she let go the loop dropped neatly over Gwen.

"Not bad," said Gwen, pulling off the noose.

Kira grinned. "I've been roping swordfish since I was Curio's age. Krill likes to make a big show of spearing them, but it's easier just to rope them and then let the crew haul them onto the deck of the ship."

Gwen looked down at her mother. "I hate to leave her here. Maybe we should just try carrying her instead of going all the way up to the laundry room for a basket."

Nikki shook her head. "It'll slow us down too much. Once we've dispatched the guard at the dungeon gate Curio and Kira can grab a laundry basket and put it on the wheeled cart we used to get down here. While they're retrieving your mother you and I will get started on my escape plan."

Gwen nodded. "Let's get to it then." She grabbed a small glass bottle off her workbench and stoppered it with a cork.

Nikki grabbed a hammer off the workbench and tucked it into her belt. Kira coiled the rope and slung it over her shoulder. Nikki led the way out of the cell and up the sloping tunnel, holding the sword in front of her. There was no sound except an occasional drip of water from the coal-black walls. She was hoping the guard at the gate would still be snoozing, but her hopes were dashed when they reached the last bend before the gate. She froze, waving the others to stop. Two men were talking nearby.

"When's yer shift end?" said one voice.

"Another two hours," said the other voice.

"Shame," said the first voice. "We're starting a dice game in the courtyard right about now. You'll miss out on a nice fat pot. The kitchen staff got paid yesterday and I plan on taking 'em for all their worth."

"Why don't we have a couple of throws right here?" said the second voice. "I got coins burning a hole in me pocket. Three throws outta five."

"Sure, why not," said the first voice. "I got no problem taking your coins before I clean out the kitchen staff."

Nikki heard the sound of dice rolling. She reached up and took down the torch burning above her head. She upended it on the damp stone floor, extinguishing it. Then she slowly crept forward until she could see around the bend. The main gate of the dungeon was still shut. Just outside the gate the guard and another man had their backs to her, intent on their dice game. She turned to the others and raised her sword.

Curio nodded and raised his comforter. Gwen un-stoppered her bottle. Kira began swinging her noose in slow circles.

Nikki waved her arm and they all rushed forward, shoving open the gate. Nikki brought the flat of her sword down on the head of the guard, knocking him out. Curio threw the comforter on top of him, rolled him into a soapy burrito, and sat on him. Kira lassoed the other man around the neck and pulled him down. Gwen splashed his face with the contents of her bottle.

It was all over in a few seconds. They stood gasping, looking at each other in astonishment at their success.

"Don't think much of the guards they got here," said Curio, poking a finger in the back of the guard he was sitting on. "We brought 'em down easier than catching hens in a chicken coop."

Nikki cut Kira's rope into pieces with her sword and they tied up the guards.

Gwen checked the pulse of both of them. "Well," she said, "at least we haven't killed anyone yet. Though this one will have some burns on his face. I panicked and used more Oil of Peace than I should have."

Nikki picked up the sword and led the way up the soapy corridor to the laundry room. As she'd expected the room was dark and deserted. A few of the giant copper vats had coals still glowing red underneath them, but the coals were safely banked for the night. She paused in the doorway and peered up the dark corridor which led to the upper floors of the tower. Very faint and far off she could hear voices, but they sounded like normal conversation. She couldn't hear any indication that an urgent search was on for her, Curio, and Kira.

"Do ya think they're missing us yet?" asked Curio, also looking up the corridor.

"It doesn't sound like it," said Nikki. "Hopefully they've restarted their card game."

Kira went over to the wheeled cart, which was still buried in the pile of wet laundry they'd crashed into. She yanked it out and gave it an experimental push.

"Seems to roll okay," she said.

"Wait a second," said Nikki, disappearing into the laundry room. She returned dragging a large wicker basket and plopped it onto the cart. "There. That should be big enough to hold Lady Ursula. You two get going. Bring her back up here as quick as you can."

Curio and Kira hopped onto the cart, skidding down the soapy corridor. Curio gave them a last wave as he disappeared around the bend into the dungeon.

"Come on," said Nikki to Gwen. "We need to hurry. We've been lucky so far, but that card game can't last forever."

"What's your plan?" asked Gwen.

"Steam," said Nikki. She headed down the soapy reed mats which ran between the large copper vats. Winding through the vats was a thick iron pipe which stretched the entire length of the room. The end of the pipe went straight through the outer wall. She banged with her knuckles on the pipe. It rang with a deep booming sound. "Hollow," she said. "It's not filled with water. I think it's above the waterline of the moat. There must be some kind of pump in here which pulls the water up from the moat and into this pipe, and then into the vats."

Gwen nodded, looking around the room. "How about over there?" she said, pointing.

"No, that's the linen room," said Nikki. "That's where Curio got his comforter." She followed the pipe back along the floor. Smaller iron pipes branched off it, each connecting to a vat. In the middle of the room the large pipe made a sudden turn and disappeared into a dark corner.

"Down here," said Nikki following the pipe to a hole in the floor. They peered into the hole. They could just make out stone steps going down into the darkness, the pipe bordering the steps on one side.

"Hang on," said Gwen. She ran to the nearest vat and tore off a piece of damp reed matting. Using the mat as a scoop she picked up two glowing pieces of coal and carried them back to where Nikki waited.

"Careful," said Gwen, starting down the stairs with the coals faintly illuminating the stone steps. "The steps are wet."

Nikki put one hand on the slimy wall to steady herself, hoping she wasn't going to fall on the sword she was carrying. As they went farther down she was surprised to see that the light was increasing. When she reached the bottom step she saw why. A huge iron furnace was pulsing away, a bed of red coals glowing through the half-open door at its base. A tank full of water hissed and boiled above the coals.

Gwen pointed to the ceiling. A thick iron pipe went up through it. "They must use the steam from the furnace as a kind of heating system for the upper floors of the tower. Quite ingenious. I've never seen anything like it in the Realm before."

Nikki noticed a series of iron wheels on one side of the furnace. "I bet these are attached to valves which shut the steam to the main pipes on and off. I doubt they use all of those laundry vats at the same time. Each one must have some kind of shut-off valve, to prevent water from flowing into it. If we shut off all the vats and block the pipe going to the upper floors I think the pressure from the steam will increase so much it'll overload the system."

Gwen looked at her worriedly. "You're trying to blow the outer wall of the tower."

Nikki nodded. "If we can get the steam pressure high enough we'll blow a hole big enough to crawl through. Then we just have to swim the moat and run for it. We'll be lost in the alleyways of Cogent Town before they know what's happening."

"An explosion like that could be hard to control," said Gwen. "We don't want to bring the roof down on our heads."

"We just need to make sure the pressure is aimed outwards, not up," said Nikki.

Gwen frowned. "I'm not sure about this. Why don't we try Kira's idea? We'll steal servant's clothes to use as a disguise. Or mother and I could hide in a laundry basket. Just cover us with sheets and push us on that cart right out the front door."

Nikki shook her head. "There's too many people wandering around on the upper floors. Servants, guards, the Count and his guests. And security is very tight at the front entrance. I'm guessing the reason they don't have many guards down here is because the front door is the only entrance to the tower. The guards there might let me or Curio out if we said that Bertie wanted us to take a message somewhere, but there's no way we can get you and your mother out that way."

"I suppose you're right," said Gwen, not sounding too happy about it. She pointed at a large iron rocker arm next to the furnace. It looked a bit like a child's seesaw. "This must be the pump which draws water in from the moat. I've seen smaller manual versions of this along the river in D-ville."

Nikki nodded. "We used to have steam pumps like this in my world, centuries ago. They were called Newcomen engines. Coal miners used to use them when the mines flooded. The furnace creates steam which causes pressure to build up in the pipes as the steam expands. When cold water is poured over a hot pipe it condenses the steam back to water, which takes up less space than steam. That creates a temporary vacuum which pulls water from the moat up using this rocker arm. We just need to close all the valves to the laundry vats, close the pipe going up to the upper floors, and then overload the furnace with coal to create enough steam pressure to blow the outer wall of the tower. I'm guessing we won't even need to blow the entire wall. That main pipe up above must be an outlet pipe, to let excess water drain back into the moat. There must be an open grate at the end of the pipe to let the water out. The steam just needs enough pressure to blow the grate."

Gwen touched a finger to the pipe running from the furnace up through the ceiling. "Burning hot," she said. "It's a bit hard to tell which wheel to turn. Well, when in doubt there's always trial and error." She turned one of the wheels on the side of the furnace all the way closed and touched the pipe again. "Nope. Not that one."

"While you're doing that I'll go up and close all the valves to the vats," said Nikki. She headed back up the stairs to the laundry room. The steamy room with its quietly glowing piles of coals was still deserted. She knelt down by a vat and peered at the joint where its feeder pipe met the bottom of the vat. Near the joint was a small iron wheel, about the size of her palm. It looked like the control to a simple gate valve. The wheel moved a metal wedge up or down to control the flow of water through the pipe. She turned the wheel all the way down. That should stop the water. She moved on to the next vat, and the next. She had closed seven valves when she heard what sounded like the rumble of far-off thunder. She poked her head over the side of the vat she was kneeling beside, squinting at the door to the laundry room. The sound was getting louder. She picked up the sword from the reed mat nearby. Were guards marching down to the dungeon? She was about to crawl back down to the furnace room to warn Gwen when a small blond head appeared in the doorway.

"Miss?" hissed Curio. "We got her."

Nikki stood up and waved.

Curio and Kira slowly pushed the wheeled cart along the soggy reed mats. Sticking out of the wicker basket was one scrawny leg encased in a dirty silk stocking.

Nikki pulled back the sheet covering Lady Ursula. She was still snoring away.

"Can you both swim?" asked Nikki.

"Like a fish," said Kira. "Some sailors can't, which always seems really stupid to me. But Griff insists that all her crew must be able to swim. Even old Posie the cook had to prove she could do the doggy paddle before Griff hired her."

"I can swim, Miss" said Curio. "But not like no fish. More like a three-legged dog that keeps going in circles. Remember, you gave me a swimming lesson after we met Mr. Warlock and his Kite Cart. I swallowed a whole lot of lake."

Nikki nodded. "Kira, you're in charge of getting Lady Ursula across the moat. Keep her in the basket. It might float. Now, help me with these valves."

The three of them quickly closed the remaining valves. Nikki had just finished the last one when Gwen appeared. She went over to the main pipe running to the outer wall and touched it.

"It's working," she said. "The pipe's getting warm."

Nikki put her palm on the pipe. "It's warm, but not hot."

"Give it time," said Gwen. "The steam will increase in pressure."

Nikki glanced over her shoulder at the door to the laundry room. "The dungeon guards will be changing shifts soon. We need to speed things up. Curio, you go help Gwen shovel more coal into the furnace. Kira, let's see what we can do about our escape route."

Nikki led Kira over to the spot where the outlet pipe went through the tower's outer wall. She was happy to see that over the years corrosion had set in. The end of the pipe was covered in rust, and the bricks around it were crumbling. She took the hammer she'd borrowed from Gwen's workbench out of her belt and tapped at the bricks. Several spots immediately turned to dust. "Here," she said, handing Kira the sword. "Go to the other side of the pipe and smash the bricks around it with the butt of the sword."

As they worked the pipe started to heat up and a banging sound ran up and down inside it.

"What's that?" asked Kira.

"It's trapped air pockets," said Nikki. "It means the pressure inside the pipe is increasing. That's what we want. Keep working on the bricks."

Gwen and Curio ran out of the furnace room. "We should be nearly there," said Gwen, feeling the pipe. "It's red hot." She pulled Kira away from the pipe. "Everyone into the corridor. We don't want to be in here when it explodes. This is not exactly a precise operation."

"You guys go," said Nikki. "Take Lady Ursula with you. I'll just smash a few more bricks. We need a hole big enough to climb through."

"No," said Gwen. "You're coming too. This isn't a controlled lab experiment. Bricks and bits of iron could fly all over the room." She grabbed Nikki's arm and dragged her away from the pipe.

Curio and Kira wheeled Lady Ursula back into the corridor and Gwen shooed them all away from the laundry room door. They waited, shooting nervous glances up and down the corridor. The banging from the pipe grew louder and louder. Suddenly the banging stopped. Nikki was about to poke her head around the door to see what was going on when Gwen suddenly shoved them all down to the ground. A huge boom shook the walls of the corridor and coal dust rained down on their heads.

"Now!" said Gwen.

They all ran back into the laundry room.

A hole the size of a well-fed cow had appeared in the tower wall. Faint moonlight shone in, illuminating a trickle of water which flowed out of the pipe and splashed into the moat below.

"Mother!" said Gwen.

"Oh, shoot!" said Curio. "Sorry, Miss. We forgot about her."

Gwen and Curio ran back for the wheeled cart while Nikki and Kira looked out of the hole in the tower wall.

"It's quite a drop," said Kira. "At least twenty feet. Too far to jump without knowing how deep the water in the moat is. It looks pretty shallow at the edge, judging by the rocks sticking out. I wish I still had that rope."

"Sheets," said Niki, running to the linen room. She returned with a pile of sheets and she and Kira tied them together. Nikki knotted them around the end of the pipe and dropped the makeshift rope out the hole. "Kira, you go first. We'll lower Lady Ursula down to you."

Kira nodded and quickly swung herself over the edge. She was down to the water's edge in no time and waved up at them.

"Pull the sheets back up," said Gwen, pushing the wheeled cart up to the hole. "We'll tie the basket to them."

Lady Ursula was heavier than she looked and it was quite a struggle to get her and the basket out of the hole and down to Kira. Unfortunately the basket promptly sank when it hit the water. Kira dived in and pulled Lady Ursula out by her hair.

"Get her across to the other side," Nikki called down. "We're right behind you."

Kira waved and put an arm around Lady Ursula's neck, backstroking across the moat.

Nikki gave Curio a boost out of the hole and he shimmied down the sheets like a capuchin monkey.

Gwen followed more slowly, the skirt of her blue silk dress tangling in the sheets. When she reached the bottom she looked like a mummy wrapped in bandages and Curio had to help untangle her.

Nikki left the hammer and the sword by the pipe. No point in trying to swim with them. She swung herself out of the hole and was soon standing next to Curio on the rocks at the edge of the moat.

"It looks a lot farther across once yer down here eye to eye with the water, don't it Miss?" he said, poking a cautious toe into the moat.

"Don't think about the distance," said Nikki. "Just take it one stroke at a time. Remember what I taught you in the lake. If you get tired turn over and float on your back."

Curio nodded and eased himself into the water. His page hat was all that was visible as he started an awkward dog paddle. The green feathers on top of his hat made him look like a strange, exotic duck out for a moonlit swim.

Nikki watched him anxiously. His progress was slow and definitely not in a straight line, but he seemed to be staying afloat. "You go next," she said to Gwen. "I'm a fast swimmer. I'll go last and keep an eye on everyone."

"This is probably not the ideal time to mention that I can't swim," Gwen said. She looked along the curving stone sides of the tower. "Maybe I can climb under the drawbridge somehow?"

"No time for that," said Nikki. "I can hear voices up there in the laundry room. Someone heard the explosion. Come on. Float on your back and I'll pull you."

"But what if I panic and drag us both down to the bottom?" said Gwen, fear shaking her voice.

"You won't panic," said Nikki. "Just stay very straight and rigid. Keep your arms out and pretend you're a piece of wood."

Gwen gave a little whimper and clenched her fists as she waded into the water. She sat back with her arms outstretched, but when the back of her head touched the water she jerked upright.

"Lay back, Gwen," Nikki snapped in her sternest Mom voice. "I can see someone looking out the hole in the tower. I think it's a servant, but the guards will soon follow. You don't want to be responsible for Kira and Curio getting caught do you? They're too young to be locked in a dungeon."

Gwen let out a strangled sound, but lay back in the water, her arms and legs out-stretched.

Nikki quickly grabbed a handful of Gwen's skirt and launched into a side-stroke, staying near Gwen's feet. She didn't want Gwen to panic and grab onto her. Even the best swimmers could be dragged under by a panicking drowning victim. Kira's technique of an arm around the throat only worked if the victim was unconscious.

"How much farther?" Gwen said in a strangled whisper.

Nikki lifted her head and took a quick look at the far bank. "Only another thirty feet or so. You're doing great." She started swimming again when suddenly she felt Gwen shift. "No!" Nikki gasped. "Don't look! Stay flat!" It was too late. Gwen had lifted her head out of the water, which broke her float position. She promptly sank under the water, her arms flailing and splashing uselessly.

Nikki dove, but it was too dark to see under the water. She grabbed blindly, hoping to catch hold of Gwen's dress, but to her dismay she felt Gwen's hand latch onto her wrist. She tried to pull free, but Gwen was older, taller, and stronger than she was. She felt Gwen try to climb onto her as if she were a life raft. Nikki couldn't push her off and they both sank to the bottom of the moat. Nikki sank up to her ankles in the mud, Gwen's feet on her shoulders pushing her down deeper into the muck. Desperate for air, Nikki clawed at Gwen's ankles. Bright spots began to flit across her eyes and she could feel herself losing consciousness. Just as she took in a mouthful of water she suddenly felt Gwen's weight lift off of her. A hand grabbed her by the arm and with startling speed yanked her to the surface.

"I think she's okay," said a deep voice as Nikki vomited up a lungful of moat water. "I've got her. You get Gwen to the bank."

"Darius?" gasped Nikki, treading water and squinting at the dark shape next to her.

"Yes," said Darius. "Quickly. We've got to get out of here before the Count's guards arrive. I can hear the drawbridge being lowered. Can you swim?"

"Yes, I'm okay," said Nikki. She swam as fast as she could to the far side of the moat, Darius beside her. A few yards in front of them a man was helping Gwen out of the water. The moonlight shone on blond hair and a scarred face. It was the Prince of Physics. He set

Gwen down on the rocks at the edge of the moat.

"Well, you certainly made a mess of the Count's tower," said the Prince, looking out across the water to where the cow-sized hole was still belching out steam.

Nikki shrugged. "We had to get out somehow," she said. "By the way, what are you doing here? I thought you were practically under house-arrest. Krill said your mansion was surrounded by the Knights of the Iron Fist."

"It was," said the Prince, squeezing water out of his velvet tunic. "We had knights at my front gate, knights peeking over my walls, and knights trampling my rose bushes. But two hours ago they all suddenly disappeared as if by magic. It took me a while to figure out what the cause was. It was something I'd not expected."

"Invaders," said Darius with a chuckle. "Practically the entire population of Kingston has come to Cogent Town. And quite a few D-ville citizens as well. All armed with rakes and pitchforks and hoes and rolling pins and frying pans."

"And don't forget the imps," said the Prince.

Darius just snorted.

The Prince gave him an angry glance. "The imps of ImpHaven have also come. Their leader is an elderly imp in a pink satin gown and a diamond tiara. She seems a match for all the knights in the Realm, the way she waves her cane around."

"That's Aunt Gertie," said Nikki. "She's a relative of Athena."

"Yes, I noticed the resemblance immediately," said the Prince. "They both have a certain imperious, steel-backboned quality. Come, let's return to my estate. It has become the unofficial headquarters of the house-cleaning."

"The what?" asked Nikki.

"The house-cleaning," said the Prince, picking up a soggy and still unconscious Lady Ursula. "It's time to cleanse the Realm from top to bottom of these unruly knights and corrupt followers of Rufius."

The Prince led the way across the jagged rocks at the edge of the moat, Curio and Kira trailing behind him. Darius offered his arm to Gwen, but she ignored him. They all scrambled over the low stone wall bordering the moat and turned to look back at the tower. Several heads were poking out of the steaming hole, shouting something at them.

"What about Mr. Bertie?" asked Curio. "He's still in there. I hope the Earl of Barbarum doesn't give him a hard time. That guy reminds me of my old master. Always ready to punch someone in the face, whether they deserve it or not."

"It's unlikely Bertie's in any danger," said the Prince. "The entire population of the Realm would rise up in fury if anyone attacked the King or the King's nephew. Rufius is very aware of this. I don't think he'll risk harming Bertie, or even holding him for ransom. Rufius's supporters in the Realm are only a tiny minority of the population and he knows it. His power is balanced on a knife edge, kept in place only by fear and bribery."

"Rufius is in there," said Nikki. "In the tower. He's at a card game with the Count and Bertie."

"I did not know that," said the Prince, peering up at the tower. "I thought he was with the King up at the castle. He hardly leaves the King's side nowadays. He gives orders the King is too lazy to give and signs documents the King is too impatient to read. Come, let us hurry. We need to gather all our allies together to determine how to knock Rufius off his knife edge of power."

# Chapter Nine

## House Cleaning

THE PRINCE'S LIBRARY was about to burst at the seams, Nikki thought, looking around at the crowd of imps, townspeople, farmers, and pirates. There were even a few nobles, standing nervously against the wall in their silk and satin finery. She spotted Lady Hyacinth talking to the Prince's butler. And she noticed Griff in a corner with her crew, the ones who'd been left behind in Lady Hyacinth's rose garden and were captured by the Knights of the Iron Fist. Krill had obviously been successful in rescuing them. Darius was standing near a bookcase full of leather-covered scrolls, glaring at every imp in the room. Even Linnea the Healer was there, chatting with others from Kingston while Rosie the mouse ran up and down her arm.

To her astonishment Nikki even spotted Mick, the scuzzy page from up at the castle who'd threatened to turn her and Curio over to the castle guards if they didn't get him a bag of gold coins. Mick was eyeing an emerald bracelet worn by one of the noblewomen. Nikki was about to go over and warn the woman when she noticed that Morton, the Prince's butler, had also spotted Mick and his sudden fascination with jewelry. Morton charged over to Mick, grabbed him by the collar of his page jacket, and dragged him out of the library.

In the center of the room, in front of the fireplace, sat the Prince of Physics, Athena, Fuzz, and Aunt Gertie. Aunt Gertie was waving her cane over her head, trying to make herself heard above the din as everyone talked at once. Fuzz was rubbing a red spot on his forehead and glaring at Aunt Gertie. He'd obviously not ducked quickly enough.

Nikki was sitting with Curio and Kira on the floor near the fire. She had a woolen blanket draped over her page uniform, which was still wet from her swim across the Count of Calumnia's moat. Gwen and Lady Ursula had been put to bed in a room upstairs. Lady Ursula was just beginning to come around, and Gwen's stomach was experiencing an unfortunate reaction to all the moat water she'd swallowed.

Morton the butler came back into the room and had a brief conversation with the Prince of Physics. The Prince nodded and stood up. He waved for silence, water still dripping from his black velvet tunic.

"Quiet, everyone," said the Prince. "I've just been informed that our scouts have seen the Knights of the Iron Fist re-grouping. They are attempting to gain control of the center of Cogent Town. They are on horseback, in full armor, and therefore a great danger to the citizens of the town. The citizens greatly outnumber them, but the Knights have the advantage in weaponry. We need to quickly form a plan which will disable them with as little loss of life as possible. There is also the problem of the Lurkers, the Rounders, and the castle guards. They have not yet made their intentions clear. We know that many of the Lurkers have been bribed by Rufius and have been doing his bidding for many months now. They are not to be trusted. The castle guards and the Rounders are more of an unknown. Both groups are more tradition-bound than the Lurkers and more loyal to the Realm and to the King. Our scouts have not yet seen any sign that the castle guards have come down from castle hill. They seem to be waiting to see how events play out down here in town. Most of the Rounders have abandoned their normal street patrols and have disappeared into their guardhouses. I doubt they will cause us much trouble, but we cannot count on any help from them either. The strange group of men from the Mystic Mountains who have been quartered up at the castle by the command of Rufius seem to have disappeared. They may have returned to their home in the mountains. Let us hope so. Now, the floor is open to ideas. One speaker at a time."

Linnea stepped forward, Rosie the mouse sitting upright on her head. "I believe I can confirm that these mountain men have left Cogent Town," she said. "I arrived here in the dead of night along with others from Kingston. As we walked the road into town we passed a large group of men dressed in odd, rough garments who spoke with an accent I have never heard before. They seemed both angry and lost at the same time. One stopped and asked me if I knew the quickest way to the Mystic Mountains. I told him that I did not, and could only suggest that they stay on the main road south toward Kingston. He said that their headman had been killed and they were returning to the mountains to bury him."

The Prince nodded. "This is good news. These strangers were acting as a bodyguard for Rufius. He is now deprived of their protection."

"I have one more thing to add," said Linnea. "I have traveled here with a group of people from Kingston who I have trained in the art of healing wounds and other injuries. Hopefully we can be of service."

"Very good," said the Prince. "I would suggest that you and your healers stay here in my house. If there are any wounded we will bring them here."

Griff stepped forward. "The Knights of the Iron Fist are dangerous, it is true. But a greater danger may be Clearwater dam. The plot to destroy the dam is known to some here. I have been to the dam and can confirm that there are marks at weak spots on the dam where a substance known as black powder could be used to bring down the entire structure. This would bring a mountainous flood of water into Cogent Town, causing immense death and destruction. We should send scouts to the dam immediately, to watch for any person approaching these weak spots. I volunteer my crew."

"So be it," said the Prince. "How many in number are your crew?"

"Twenty good men," said Griff.

"You may need more," said the Prince. "The Knights may try to prevent you from reaching the dam. Are there any here willing to go also?"

A nobleman in a purple satin tunic stepped forward. "I will go with this pirate. I have a large estate in Clearwater Gardens, near the dam. I will gather the men from my household and others from nearby estates who are loyal to the King."

"Make sure you gather my gardeners," called Lady Hyacinth. "They are a sight to be seen when they wield their lawn scythes. My head gardener could swipe a knight's head clean off his shoulders, armor or no armor."

The Prince nodded and the nobleman left the room, followed by Griff and her crew. The Prince had just started to speak again when a huge boom suddenly shook the windows of the library. The chandelier hanging from the ceiling swung back and forth like a pendulum.

"The cannons!" Nikki cried. "We forgot about the Count of Calumnia's cannons!" She jumped up and ran to a window. Her view was obscured by the lilac bushes in the Prince's front garden, but she could see a plume of smoke rising into the air.

"That looks like it hit the market square, Miss," said Curio, standing on his tiptoes next to her. "Good thing not many folks are at the stalls this time of night. I wonder if it missed its target or if that was just a warning shot."

"We'll know in only a few minutes," said the Prince of Physics, looking out of a nearby window. "It takes a trained crew only five minutes to load and fire a cannon."

The entire room was still as everyone waited in horrified silence for the next explosion. All eyes were on a grandfather clock near the windows as its brass pendulum swung back and forth, ticking off the minutes.

Nikki left the window and sat down at a writing desk in a corner of the library. She pulled a piece of parchment from its top drawer and dipped a quill in a silver inkpot. "Projectile motion," she muttered under her breath. The motion of a cannonball could be modelled by a parabolic equation. To find the distance a cannonball could travel you solved for the horizontal value. The acceleration of gravity on the earth's surface was always the same, -9.8 meters per second squared, but she'd have to estimate the other variables. The equation would be $s = ut - 1/2gt^2$, with u being the initial velocity of the cannonball and t being time. Solving for s would give the distance the cannonball could travel. She estimated that the travel time of the cannonball's flight was less than five seconds. The initial velocity was more difficult. She vaguely remembered a question on a trig test from two years ago about cannonballs and parabolic motion. The initial velocity had been about 200 meters per second. She solved the equation using a variety of initial velocities, then waved Curio over.

"Yes, Miss?" asked Curio.

"How far is the Count of Calumnia's tower from this house?" asked Nikki.

"About a league, maybe a little less," said Curio.

"How long is a league?" asked Nikki.

"About five thousand feet," said Curio.

Nikki breathed a sigh of relief. Five thousand feet was a bit less than a mile. All her calculations showed that a cannonball launched from the Calumnia tower would travel a maximum of about 1,000 feet. The initial velocity would be affected by the strength of the gunpowder used, but as the Count's guards were most likely using Geber's older, weaker type of black powder the distance was probably even shorter. It was very unlikely a cannonball could hit the Prince's mansion.

"How far is the market square from the Count of Calumnia's tower?" asked Nikki.

"I'd guess about a quarter of a league, Miss," said Curio.

"So, that's about 1,200 feet," said Nikki. "These are some estimates of how far the Count's cannons can shoot," she said, pointing at the parchment. "I'd say that the market square is at about maximum range for the cannons. If we evacuate everyone from the buildings closer to the tower than 1,200 feet they should be safe. At least from the cannons. Maybe not from the dam bursting or from the Knights of the Iron Fist, but one problem at a time. I'll let the Prince know so he can devise an evacuation plan."

Curio nodded, staring down at Nikki's hastily scribbled equations. "Can I have that, Miss?" he asked.

"The parchment?" asked Nikki in surprise. "Sure, I guess. But we don't need it anymore."

"I just wants it for a keepsake," said Curio, folding the piece of parchment and stuffing it inside his page jacket.

Nikki shrugged. She wasn't sure if she was introducing new mathematical concepts into the Realm, but she didn't have time to ponder the issue. She was always wary of bringing new ideas and technology into the Realm, but right now saving lives was more important. She rose from the desk as the Prince returned to the center of the room.

"Ample time to re-load has passed," said the Prince. "It would seem that was just a warning shot. If their aim was to unleash a multitude of shots they would have done so by now. We know that Rufius is with the Count of Calumnia. The Count has a ring of cannons on top of his tower. He has always insisted that they are just historical artifacts left over from earlier times and are not used anymore. Obviously he was lying. My guess is that Rufius ordered a single cannon shot to be fired to instill fear into the citizens of Cogent Town. People will be on edge, not certain what to do or where to go. It seems Rufius is trying to control them using three threats. Armed knights surrounding the town, the menace of Clearwater dam breaking, and finally destruction by cannon fire. Griff and her crew have been sent to watch the dam. That leaves the other two threats."

"The imps will see to the knights," said Aunt Gertie, standing on her chair and swinging her cane over her head. "Nets! That's what's needed. We've brought wagon loads of fishing nets from Kingston. They worked a treat when those iron-clad rascals invaded ImpHaven. Throw a net over one and drag him from his horse! Watch him squirm on the ground like a codfish gasping for air on the beach!"

"We volunteer to join the imps in this plan," said a farmer from Kingston, banging his pitchfork on the floor. "I raise corn and pigs nowadays, but in my youth I hauled in the codfish catches on many a ship. I can throw a net with the best of them."

The Prince nodded. "This threat from the Knights of the Iron Fist will need many volunteers. Our scouts have counted roughly three hundred knights in town. Any who are strong enough to throw a net and willing to go, follow this brave farmer and this brave imp."

The Prince helped Aunt Gertie down from her chair and she and the farmer left the library at the head of a cheering crowd of imps, farmers, fishermen and a few clerks from Deceptionville with ink-stained fingers who looked extremely nervous.

Fuzz stood up and gave the startled Athena a kiss on the cheek. "See you soon, old girl," he said. "Look after yourself. I'll keep an eye on your Aunt Gertie, though she'll probably do me in long before the Knights have a chance." He gave the Prince a jaunty salute and followed after the imps.

After the net-throwers had left only a few people remained in the room. Gwen slipped in through the open door. She had changed out of her sodden blue silk gown and was wearing a cotton dress with a daisy print which was too short for her.

"Now," said the Prince. "The cannons."

"I have some ideas about how to destroy them," said Nikki. "But they'll be very hard to reach, especially now that we've blown a hole in the Count of Calumnia's tower. His guards will be on high alert."

Athena stirred in her chair. She was still very sickly and her wounded leg was stretched out on a footstool. "I believe we may be able to make use of the old coal baskets," she said.

"Of course!" said the Prince. "One of the coal lines stretches right above the Count of Calumnia's tower. Though I'm not sure if it's still in use. After so many of those old baskets broke and dropped coal onto people's heads most of the coal lines were cut down."

"What are coal baskets?" asked Nikki.

"An old way of transporting coal from the mines north of Cogent Town to people's houses," said Athena. "The mines were high up in the hills. Metal wires were strung down the hills on tall wooden poles and baskets full of coal could slide all the way to town. Some of the richest families had their own coal lines delivering baskets straight to their mansions. It was a fast but unreliable way to transport coal. It was difficult to control the speed of the baskets and sometimes they would slam into houses and scatter coal all over the street. Nowadays we use horse-drawn wagons to bring the coal into town."

"Are you saying we should ride in these coal baskets?" asked Nikki.

Athena shook her head. "I doubt any of the baskets still exist. But many of the metal wires are still in place. Children sometimes play on them. They throw a rope over the lines closest to the ground and slide down them. I myself am not fond of such antics, but Fuzz has used the lines on occasion. I remember him telling me only last year about using a line near the Calumnia tower to escape from some ruffians. I learned later that they were not in fact ruffians but were tavern owners chasing Fuzz for not paying his gambling debts."

"And one of these lines goes right over the Count's tower?" asked Nikki.

"Right to its top, I believe," said Athena. "The coal used to be dumped on the roof."

"But even if you manage to reach the roof of the tower you'll be seen," said the Prince. "The Count's guards are stationed on the roof. Their guardhouse is located there. And also their cannons. The Count has shown me the roof in years past. He has quite a formidable defense. I don't remember the exact number, but he has a multitude of large cannons, arranged in a circle in all directions, pointed at both Cogent Town and at Castle Cogent."

"We'll wait until the moon sets," said Nikki. "That should be in an hour or so. During the darkest part of the night we should be hard to spot as we slide along the wires."

"Yes, but the guards on top of the tower will see you once you reach the roof," said the Prince.

"I can help with that," said Gwen, coming forward. "I know of a substance which can create billowing clouds which will hide us from view. You should have the necessary ingredients here in this house. The guards will know something is up, but we will still have some advantage of surprise."

"I'll deal with the guards once we're on top of the tower," said Krill.

"And I," said Darius from his corner near the bookcase.

The Prince looked at them somberly. "This is a very dangerous undertaking. We do not know how many guards are stationed on the roof of the tower. They could be too numerous for only two men to handle. I would go with you, but I feel I should stay here and warn the people of Cogent Town of the dangers they face. We may have to evacuate the town."

"I will go with them," said Gwen. "I have a liquid which can disable a man when thrown in his face."

At this the Prince looked even more grave, but he nodded reluctantly. "So be it. You three head for the tower and attempt to disable the Count's cannons."

"I'm going too." said Nikki.

"Absolutely not," said the Prince. "You will stay here and help the healers." He pointed at Nikki, Kira, and Curio. "All three of you will stay here. I am not sending children to battle armed guards."

Nikki opened her mouth to protest, but the Prince turned his back on her and led Gwen, Krill, and Darius out of the library.

"Cheer up young Nikki," said Linnea the Healer. "I'll find plenty for you and your friends to do. Come, let's see what the Prince's linen closets can provide. You three can start tearing up his sheets for bandages."

✦　✦　✦　✦

"OUCH!" HISSED KIRA. "You're standing on my head!"

"Sorry," whispered Nikki. She lifted her feet and hung by her hands from the ivy vine growing on the side of the Prince's mansion. "I can't see anything it's so dark. Where's Curio?"

"Already down, Miss," whispered Curio from the lawn in the Prince's back garden.

Nikki half climbed, half slid down the rest of the ivy and joined Curio and Kira on the lawn. A few windows glowed above their heads with faint candlelight, but otherwise the house and its grounds were dark and still.

"Over here, Miss," whispered Curio. "This is the spot where Krill climbed over the wall and escaped from the knights."

Nikki felt the rough stones of the wall. It was twice her height and had no convenient vines to provide handholds. She tried to pull herself up it, only to slide back down, bumping her chin painfully on the stones.

"You gotta dig yer fingers into the cracks," whispered Curio. He managed to climb a few feet, but then slipped off, falling with a thump onto the lawn.

"I've got a better idea," whispered Kira. She climbed up into an apple tree near the back wall of the garden and tied the rope she was carrying to a branch. Then she swung from the tree to the top of the wall. She teetered for a second and Nikki and Curio rushed forward to catch her, but she managed to get her balance. She dropped the rope back down to the lawn. Curio wrap the end of it around his shoulder and climbed with it up the apple tree. His first swing wasn't a success and he slammed into the side of the wall, letting out a tiny whimper.

"Are you all right?" whispered Nikki.

"Just fine, Miss," he gasped, sliding down the rope.

"I'll give you a push," whispered Nikki. "That should give you enough momentum."

They both climbed the tree. Curio grasped the rope with both hands and Nikki pushed him as hard as she could. This time he cleared the top of the wall, but swung so fast that he whizzed by Kira and headed back toward the apple tree. Kira grabbed the rope on his return swing and managed to stop him in mid-flight. Curio shimmed down the rope and joined her on top of the wall.

Nikki soon joined them, managing a successful swing with only a slightly banged knee. She kept hold of the rope and dropped it down the far side of the wall. The three of them climbed down it to the dark alley between the Prince's mansion and his neighbor.

"Curio you lead the way," whispered Nikki. "You know Cogent Town the best."

"Okay, Miss," whispered Curio. "Follow close. I knows some back ways and narrow alleys that knights on horseback won't be able to fit through. They'd get stuck like a fat D-ville merchant trying to put on his schoolboy pants."

Curio led them the long way around, doubling back and weaving to and fro. They climbed over hedges and ducked under hanging laundry and trampled flowerbeds and started all the dogs in town furiously barking, but eventually they arrived back at the Count of Calumnia's tower. They peered over the low wall surrounding the moat. Steam was still hissing out of the hole they'd made. Someone had covered the hole with a white sheet. The sheet flapped and billowed in the breeze like the jib of a sailboat heading into a storm.

"Don't see the point of the sheet," said Curio. "How's that gonna stop anybody?"

"I think it's mostly psychological," said Nikki. "Bricking up a hole that big takes time, so they just patched it with the first thing they could find." She looked worriedly at Curio. "Are you sure you can handle this?" she asked.

Curio patted her shoulder. "Don't worry about me, Miss." He brushed a smudge of dirt off his page jacket and fluffed the still damp feather on top of his hat. "They knows somebody made that hole, but they don't know who. And them guards in the dungeon never saw us. We knocked 'em clean out before they got a glimpse. And with this outfit I'm still under Mr. Bertie's protection, so to speak. I'll just give 'em a story about how we three ran away cause we was scared when that fight broke out in the card room. Pretty easy story to believe, as lots of people are scared of that crazy Earl of Barbarum." He pulled his hat low over his face and disappeared into the darkness in the direction of the tower's drawbridge.

"That kid is something else," said Kira, settling cross-legged on the ground with the moat wall against her back. "I've met a few pedestal babies, and they're all pretty tough. They have to be, what with their parents abandoning them on a stone pedestal in D-ville. A lot of them go bad. They steal food cause they have no choice, and no one faults them for that. But then they get stuck in kind of a stealing rut. Lots move onto worse things as they get older. Robbing and beating people, even murder. They're not all bad, but I've never met one like Curio. He can out chipper a chipmunk, and he's so polite all the time, despite not having no family. Me and Krill, at least we've got each other. And Griff treats us like family. Makes me feel very lucky. When this mess in Cogent Town is over maybe I'll ask Griff if she'll take Curio on as part of the crew."

"That'd be nice," said Nikki. "But I'm not sure he'd accept. Somehow I can't see Curio as a pirate, or a cod fisherman. He's got a really strong interest in book-learning, or scroll-learning as he'd call it. I think he'd be better off in an alchemist's shop, like the one Gwen worked at in Deceptionville. There'd be a lot for him to learn, and he could work his way up to chief alchemist or something. I wouldn't want him working for Avaricious of course, but there must be a few shop owners who aren't crooks."

Kira nodded. "You're probably right. Well, we can arrange Curio's future when things have gotten back to normal. Are you good to keep watch? I could use a bit of a snooze."

"Go ahead," said Nikki. "I'm too wound up to sleep."

That turned out not to be the case. Nikki found herself jerking awake, stretched out on the cobblestones and uncertain where she was. Kira was snoring gently beside her and the sound of running feet was approaching out of the darkness.

"Get up! Quick!" hissed Curio, running up to them, his breath coming in harsh gasps. "I got it but they're hot on my heels!"

Nikki jumped up, dragging Kira up with her. "Which way?" she asked, looking wildly around.

"Follow me," gasped Curio. "It's not far, but we gotta lose 'em first."

Nikki could hear shouts behind them as they raced across the deserted fish market they'd crossed in Bertie's carriage that afternoon. She slipped on a fish head and nearly fell. Kira grabbed her arm just in time.

"Duck, Miss!" hissed Curio, diving into a drainage pipe on the edge of the market. It was barely two feet in diameter and dark sludge was oozing out of it.

Nikki crawled in after him, the slimy sides of the pipe closing in around her with only inches to spare. She squirmed along on her stomach, pulling herself along by her elbows. She could see nothing at all. Ahead of her Curio's feet kept splashing muddy, fishy water into her face. The stench was so bad that it was all Nikki could do not to vomit. After what seemed hundreds of yards she emerged from the pipe, spitting up foul water and rubbing her painfully banged-up elbows.

"Where are we?" gasped Kira, emerging from the pipe and clutching her ribcage. The long rope she'd been carrying was tangled around her head and shoulders.

"We're at the bottom of the Castle Hill Crags, Miss," said Curio. "That's what the locals call this area. These crags is too steep to build on, so the houses end here. You can just make out the road up to Castle Cogent over there. There's guards posted at the bottom of the road, but they never post guards here by the crags. They're not really needed. The crags is too steep to climb. People try sometimes, on a dare or when they're drunk. The dares break an arm or a leg, the drunks break their necks."

Nikki peered around, her eyes adjusting to the faint moonlight. They were in a narrow cleft in the crags, with rocky cliffs rising high above their heads. The pipe they'd squirmed through trickled filthy water around their feet. She bent and squinted into the pipe. "Unless the Count of Calumnia hires ten-year-old kids there's no way anyone's followed us. A grown man couldn't possibly fit through that pipe."

"No, Miss," said Curio. "And they didn't see us go in. I checked. It's not likely they know where we are." He un-looped a canvas bag hanging from his shoulders and handed it to Nikki. "I got as much as I could find, Miss. Didn't see any more stashed in Miss Gwen's cell. I searched the whole cell real quick-like, but I didn't want to stay too long. The dungeon was empty but I could hear guards talking in the laundry room."

Nikki opened the top of the bag and coughed as the pungent smell of gunpowder hit her nose. She hefted the bag. "You got quite a lot. More than I expected. This has to be at least five pounds of powder. It should be enough to destroy all of the Count's cannons. I'm surprised the guards at the drawbridge let you take it out of the tower."

"They didn't see it, Miss," said Curio. "I stuffed it down my jacket and bent over like I had the stomach ache. I even pretended to upchuck on one of the guard's feet. They couldn't get rid of me fast enough. I thought I'd fooled 'em, and I was safe across the draw-bridge when all of a sudden there was a ruckus behind me and the guards started chasing me. Don't know why. Maybe they had new orders."

Kira was running her hands over the base of the rocky crags. "I suppose you're going to tell us we have to climb these," she said.

"Afraid so, Miss," said Curio. "It won't be easy, but yer rope will help." He pointed to a sharp finger-like shaft of rock far above their heads. "See that point, Miss? If you can rope it the way you did the guard in the dungeon then we'll have it much easier. That point's not far from the coal wire I'm aiming for."

Kira nodded and un-looped the long rope from her shoulder. She took a few practice swings. "It's not gonna be easy. There's not a lot of space here to swing the rope. I need to whirl it in circles to get up enough speed." Her first attempt to lasso the shaft fell far short. Kira tried a few more times, but finally shook her head. "Nope, there just isn't enough space in this tight cleft. I'm gonna have to climb up to that shelf up there. If I stand on that I'll have a clear space to swing the rope." She re-wound the rope around her shoulder.

Nikki watched with clenched hands as Kira started to climb. The rocks were nearly vertical, with shard-like fragments which broke under Kira's grip and tumbled down like tiny avalanches. Kira slipped many times, sometimes hanging by only one hand. Nikki and Curio hovered underneath her, but they knew that the higher she climbed the more unlikely it was they'd be able to break her fall.

Finally Kira managed to haul herself up onto the flat shelf of rock. She knelt for a minute to catch her breath, then stood and braced her feet wide apart. She swung the rope in wider and wider circles, making a buzzing sound in the night air. Then with a whiplash motion too fast for the eye to see she launched the circle of rope straight up. It flew through the air, higher and higher until it dropped light as a feather over the finger-like shaft of rock far above Kira's head. Kira slowly pulled on the rope until the loop was tight around the shaft. Then she dropped the excess rope down toward Nikki and Curio. It hung a few feet from the ground.

"One at a time," Kira called down to them. "This rope's pretty strong, but I don't know if it'll hold both of you. The Prince had stronger ropes in his garden shed, but I picked this one for its length."

Curio went first, scrambling up the rope like a tiny monkey. Nikki looped the bag of black powder over her shoulders and followed more slowly. The rope made the climb much easier, but her arms were aching as she joined Curio on the sharp finger of rock.

Kira joined them, hauling up the excess rope.

"There it is, Miss," said Curio, pointing to a spot only ten feet above their heads. "It's hard to see, but it flashes when the moonlight hits it."

Nikki soon spotted it, a long silvery thread hanging from the crags. The flashes extended all the way across the fish market, across the Count of Calumnia's moat, and ended at the very top of his tower. The angle of the line was steeper than she'd expected. She wondered if they'd be able to slow themselves down before crashing into the brick crenellations at the top of the tower.

"We need some kind of brake," she said to Kira. "Our feet might help. We could rub them against the line to slow us down. Can you cut us some lengths for both our hands and feet?"

Kira nodded and pulled out the fish-boning knife she always carried. She cut a length of rope four feet long. "This should be long enough for our hands. Just throw the rope over the coal line and hang on tight to each end. She cut a shorter length. "Put this on the line first and tie the two ends together. Then hang one foot inside the loop. If you're going too fast just lift your foot and rub your shoe against the line. But don't do it too soon or you might not make it to the top of the tower."

Nikki nodded, peering down at the top of the Calumnia tower. She didn't see any lights or movement, but she could just make out the dark shapes of the cannons forming a ring around the outer edge. A stone building she assumed was the guardhouse was in the center of the ring. She listened carefully for any shouts coming from the tower, but could hear nothing but the harsh caw of a raven nearby. "I wonder if Gwen, Krill, and Darius are still planning their attack," she said. "I don't see any sign of them on the top of the tower."

"We'd better wait then," said Kira. "I get that you have an idea about using that powder to destroy the cannons, but the three of us swinging down the coal line into the middle of a bunch of guards is not gonna go well."

"Yes, you're right," said Nikki. "We should wait." She glanced up. The steep, rocky crags led to the gleaming marble walls of Castle Cogent far above. "I don't see any other coal lines," she said. "Do you think they've found another way in?"

"They could be trying the tunnels, Miss," said Curio. "Miss Gwen said she knew the layout of the coal mines round here from her maps. They could maybe sneak into the Count's dungeons that way."

Nikki frowned. "That sounds awfully dangerous. They'd need to get all the way from the dungeons to the top of the tower without being seen."

"Maybe they think they can fight their way to the top," said Kira. "Either way we need to wait. We'll be useless if they can't take out the guards first."

The three of them settled as comfortably as they could on the sharp point of rock. Every now and then faint cries rang out in the night. In the distance a clash of steel on steel could be heard, and horses' hooves pounded along the cobblestone streets.

"Look, Miss," said Curio, pointing down at the fish market.

A small band of imps had run into the square, the sound of hooves close behind. The imps quickly spread a large fishing net on the ground, keeping hold of its edges. When a knight in full armor charged into the square and rode right over the net the imps suddenly pulled it off the ground. The net entangled the legs of the knight's horse and both horse and rider crashed to the ground. The knight was caught underneath the flailing animal. The imps rushed forward and wound the fishing net around and around him. He struggled furiously, then suddenly went limp.

Nikki looked away.

"They got 'im, Miss," said Curio. "Can't rightly tell if they done him in. Wouldn't blame them if they did. Them knights did horrible things in ImpHaven, so they say."

"Look!" said Kira suddenly, pointing to the tower. "That must be Gwen's smoke. They've made it to the top."

A cloud of thick white smoke billowed out from the top of the tower, blocking their view of the cannons.

"We'll just have to hope it's them," said Nikki. "I can't see anything at all. There could be hundreds of guards up there, or none at all."

"I don't think the Count of Calumnia has hundreds of guards," said Kira. "A few dozen at the most, I'd guess." She gathered up the lengths of rope she'd cut and hung them around her neck. "Come on. Let's get this over with. All this waiting is getting to me."

They climbed the last ten feet up to the old coal line. It was a metal line attached to the rock face with what looked to Nikki like a huge iron staple. She reached out and tugged on the line. It felt solid and taut, but its surface was surprisingly rough. "We need to wrap the ropes," she said. "This line feels like it could cut right through them."

Kira braced herself against the rock face and pulled out her fish knife. "Take off one of your shoes," she said. She pulled off one of her own boots and sliced at it with her knife. The sharp boning knife quickly reduced the boot to strips of leather. Kira wrapped the middle section of one rope with the leather strips and tested the wrapped portion against the coal wire. "That should hold until we make it to the tower. We can use the foot which still has its shoe to slow us down."

"Okay," said Kira once all the ropes were ready. "I'm going first."

"No, I'll go first," said Nikki.

Kira shook her head. "I'm the oldest and tallest. I'm also good with a knife. I stand the best chance if we reach the tower and run smack into any armed guards." Before Nikki could argue Kira threw a rope over the coal line and quickly tied a loop in it. She stuck her foot in the loop, threw the hand-rope with its leather wrap over the line and tightly grasped its ends. She took a deep breath and pushed off the rocky crag with her free foot. Her slide down the metal wire was startlingly fast. She whizzed over the fish market, sped across the moat, and approached the tower at such blinding speed that Nikki was sure she was going to crash.

At the last minute Nikki could see sparks shooting off of Kira. She was using her leather boot to brake. She slid over the top of the tower's crenellations and disappeared from view.

Nikki readied her own ropes then turned to Curio. "Maybe you should stay here," she said. "If there are too many armed guards . . ."

Curio folded his scrawny arms and gave her an odd look, half stubborn, half amused. "Miss, how exactly are you gonna stop me?"

he asked.

Nikki sighed. "Fair point," she said and pushed off. The speed of the slide took her breath away. There was no time to be scared. The top of the tower approached so fast she almost forgot to brake. She barely got her foot on the coal line before she shot over the crenellations and into a heavy white fog where nothing was visible.

# Chapter Ten

━━◗●◖━━

## Fire and Water

"KIRA?" NIKKI WHISPERED into the fog.

No answer. She picked herself up off the ground and rubbed her foot. The speed of her descent had burned right through her leather shoe and scorched her skin. She took a step forward and walked right into what felt like a giant bale of hay. A strong smell of coal wafted from it. Nikki guessed that the hay bale was there to slow down the baskets of coal when the line had still been in use. She was thankful it was still there. She'd come over the top of the tower way too fast. Crashing into the hay bale had probably saved her life. She didn't want to think about what would have happened if she'd crashed into the stone walls of the tower at that speed. Suddenly she noticed a buzzing sound behind her. She ducked just in time.

"Aaaah!" cried Curio as he slammed into the hay bale and fell to the ground.

Nikki helped him up.

"Oh, Miss," whispered Curio. "It feels like my foot is burned clean off."

"Let me see," Nikki whispered, kneeling down. Between the darkness of the night and the thick fog she could barely see Curio's shoe. Strips of what she hoped was leather were hanging from it. When she touched the shoe her fingers became coated with blood.

Curio moaned.

"Can you wiggle your toes?" asked Nikki.

"Yes, Miss," Curio gasped in a strangled voice.

"Good," whispered Nikki. "It looks like a nasty cut, but I don't think it's a severe injury." She pulled the stocking off of her shoeless foot and wrapped it around the cut. "Lean on me."

Curio put his arm around her shoulder and Nikki half-dragged him over to the stone wall of the tower. She set him down.

"Stay here," she said. "Keep low. I need to find Kira. And I need to find the others if they're here."

"I don't hear no fighting, Miss," whispered Curio. "Seems like a good sign."

"Yes it does," Nikki whispered. She didn't say what she was thinking. That the fighting was over because Gwen, Krill and Darius had been killed by the Count's guards. She crept slowly around the circular outer wall of the tower, listening carefully. She could hear far-off sounds of fighting down on the streets of Cogent Town, but up on the tower nothing stirred. Every ten feet or so she had to duck down under the barrel of a cannon pointed out toward the town. The bag of gunpowder was still on her back, but she didn't want to put her plan into action until she'd found Kira and the others.

She stepped on the body before she saw it. She jerked her foot back in horror. The man was dressed in the Count of Calumnia's livery. A tower guard. He was face down, with blood pooling around his head. Nikki forced herself to step over him and continue. She found two more dead guards before she circled all the way back to Curio.

"Is it all clear, Miss?" whispered Curio.

Nikki was about to answer when her stomach suddenly reacted to the horrors. She leaned over the crenellations and vomited. She felt Curio pat her shoulder.

"It's okay, Miss," he said. "Sit down for a sec and tell me what's up."

Nikki wiped her mouth on her sleeve. "Three dead guards," she said. "I didn't see anyone else. I don't know where Kira's gone to. It doesn't seem likely that she'd go down into the tower."

"She might have," said Curio. "If she thought her brother was down there."

"I haven't checked inside the guardhouse yet," said Nikki. "Its door was open, but there weren't any sounds coming from it."

"Let's go check together, Miss," said Curio.

They slowly approached the stone building in the center of the tower, Curio limping and leaning on Nikki's arm. At the doorway Nikki gently released his grip and went through the door alone. It was very dark, but the fog was less thick than outside. As her eyes adjusted to the faint light from the narrow windows she spotted two more guards lying on the floor.

"In the corner, Miss," Curio said in a barely audible whisper.

Nikki looked where he was pointing and froze. Something was moving in the darkness. It was swaying back and forth, a very faint moaning sound coming from it.

Together Nikki and Curio slowly approached it. The dim shape resolved into a woman. Her pale dress was covered in blood and she was shaking with silent sobs.

It was Gwen.

Nikki knelt down beside her.

Gwen didn't seem to notice. She was cradling a body in her arms. Darius.

"I'm so sorry, Gwen," said Nikki.

Gwen didn't respond.

"Gwen, are you hurt?" asked Nikki.

No response.

Nikki felt Darius's neck for a pulse, but it was as she feared. He was dead.

"There don't seem to be nobody else here, Miss," said Curio. "Only place Miss Kira and Mr. Krill could have gone is down into the tower."

Nikki nodded. "Curio, can you walk well enough to get to the cannons?" she asked.

"Of course, Miss," said Curio. "I'll just hop on one foot."

Nikki unhooked the bag of gunpowder from her back. "Take this. Pour a bit into the muzzle of each cannon and use a ramrod to tamp it in. I saw ramrods lying next to most of the cannons. If there's any powder left go around again until it's gone. Then go back to the hay bale we crashed into and find our ropes. Start pulling them apart. I need long threads I can tie together into one long fuse. While you're doing that I'm going to go down into the tower and try to find Kira and Krill."

"Got it, Miss," said Curio. He gave Gwen a soft little pat on the shoulder and hopped out of the guardhouse.

"Gwen," said Nikki. "I need to go, but I'll come back for you."

Gwen didn't respond.

Nikki left the guardhouse. It wasn't immediately obvious how to get off the roof of the tower. She stumbled around in the dark, tripping over piles of cannon balls. Finally she found the entrance to the roof by nearly falling into it. It was a steep stone stairway slanting down to the lower floors. She hurried down it, wondering why she wasn't encountering anyone. Surely the Count of Calumnia had more guards. Maybe they knew what had happened to the others and were hiding down below, afraid to return to the roof. She reached the level below the roof. Its floor slanted downward and spiraled around the tower just like when they'd followed Bertie to the card game. This level had no rooms branching off the slanting hallway. She'd gone two turns around the spiral when she suddenly spotted firelight glancing off the stone walls. She could hear men yelling something and a girl screaming something in return. It was Kira.

Nikki ran around the bend of the spiral, ready to rush to Kira's aid, but the scene that met her eyes froze her in place.

Kira was sheltering behind a stack of powder kegs, Krill's limp body stretched out on the stones at her feet. Twenty feet farther on an iron portcullis was blocking the way down. Its iron rungs were sunk deep into holes in the stone floor. A cluster of tower guards on the other side of the portcullis was trying without success to push it open or pull it up. In the middle of the crush of guards was the hideously enraged face of the Earl of Barbarum. He was shouting obscenities at Kira and throwing rocks at the stack of powder kegs. The knives he had thrown at her were stuck deep into the wood of the kegs.

Nikki noticed a slight movement behind the crush of guards at the portcullis. Rufius. He was standing well back from the others, holding a flaming torch. Nikki wasn't surprised to see that he was still in the tower. It was probably the safest place to be right now, what with all the fighting in the streets of Cogent Town.

Nikki ducked as a rock whizzed by her head. The Earl had noticed her. She dropped to her knees and crawled behind the pile of powder kegs. "Is he . . ." she asked, laying a hand on Krill's arm.

Kira shook her head. "No. He's alive. There's a deep gash on his back, probably from a sword. He was conscious until a few moments ago. I think it's the blood loss that made him collapse."

Nikki felt for the pulse in Krill's neck. Yes, he was still alive.

"I found him here behind the powder kegs. I think he was going down to the lower floors to look for Bertie," said Kira.

"Did you drop the portcullis?" asked Nikki.

"No," said Kira. "It was down when I got here. The mechanism which controls it looks like it was smashed by a hammer. I think Darius lowered it. It certainly wasn't the tower guards. They've been trying like mad to raise it."

Nikki sunk her head into her hands, trying to think. Her plan had been to destroy the cannons using the bag full of Gwen's gunpowder.

It was likely much stronger than the powder the guards had. The combination of stronger powder plus pouring too much into each cannon should cause the cannon's barrels to burst. It was possible the explosions would be so strong that the roof of the tower would be destroyed. She'd planned to lead everyone down to the laundry room and escape through the hole they'd made. But with Darius dead and Krill unconscious this was going to be impossible. It was a long way down the spiral to the laundry room. She'd been counting on Darius and Krill to fight through any guards they encountered.

"Oh no," gasped Kira. "Look!"

Nikki looked where she was pointing. Rufius had set his flaming torch on the stone floor and was stringing an arrow into a bow. He dipped the arrowhead into the torch and it burst into flame.

"The powder kegs!" gasped Nikki. "He's going to explode them!" She scrambled to her feet and grasped one of Krill's arms. Kira grabbed the other and they pulled him away from the powder kegs as fast as they could. They had just managed to round the bend up the spiral ramp when the stone walls of the tower shook and bits of rock rained down on their heads.

"Keep going!" Nikki shouted. "I need to see if the portcullis is still blocking their way."

Kira shouted something, but Nikki ignored her and kept running. If the guards managed to get through the portcullis their situation was hopeless.

The air was thick with powder, ash, and slivers of wood. Nikki covered her mouth and nose with her sleeve. The spot where the powder kegs had stood was now a gaping hole. She could see through the stone floor into the level below. To her great relief the iron portcullis was still intact. It was bent in places where flying stones had hit it, but all of the guards were still on the other side. Several of them were lying on the floor, hit by the stones. Rufius was standing over them, ignoring their pleas for help. His black tunic, always oddly immaculate, was completely free of powder and ash. When he spotted her he strung another arrow on his bow.

Nikki pivoted and ran as fast as she could back up the slanting hallway. She caught up to Kira at the bottom of the stairs to the roof.

"They're still blocked by the portcullis," she said. "At least for now. They might have more powder they could use to blow it, or a blacksmith might be able to melt some of the rungs. But that will take time. We should have just enough time to destroy the cannons and escape."

"Escape how?" asked Kira. "There's no way down."

"The coal line," said Nikki. "It's still intact. If we can pull ourselves up it, just to the moat, then we can drop into the water. We won't have to go far up, maybe twenty feet. The tower is very close to the moat."

Kira looked down at Krill, lying at her feet. "He won't be able to climb."

"We'll make some kind of harness for him," said Nikki. "Gwen will have some ideas. She's in shock because of Darius, but if you can get her to see that Krill's life depends on her that might bring her out of it. She's in the guardhouse. Leave Krill down here. We'll all need to come down here when I light the gunpowder."

Nikki dashed up the stairs. Some of the fog had lifted and a crescent moon was rising over Castle Cogent high above. She ran over to the hay bale. Curio was seated next to it, pulling long threads of hemp out of their coal line ropes.

"Great job," said Nikki, snatching up the threads and knotting them end to end. "We have to hurry. Darius brought down an iron portcullis on the level below and it's blocking anyone else from coming up on the roof. That's bought us some time, but not much. They'll get through eventually."

Curio nodded. "I got all them cannons loaded," he said. "Used up the whole bag of powder."

"Good," said Nikki. "I'm creating one long fuse. We'll light the end of it and go down the stairs. We don't want to be up here when the blast goes off. I'm not sure how powerful it will be. It might take down some of the crenellations or flatten the guardhouse."

"Save some of those ropes," said Gwen from behind them. Her white dress was soaked in blood and she was swaying on her feet, but her eyes were clear and intent. "I'll need at least two ropes to hold Krill's shoulders and legs. We can cut them once he's over the water."

Nikki nodded. "Kira and I will go up the coal line first. We're the best swimmers. We'll need to be in the water before Krill is dropped. Once we get him to the surface Kira can pull him to the other side of the moat. I'll dive for you once we've got Krill."

"I can help Miss Gwen," said Curio. "I'm getting good at the poodle paddle."

"The dog paddle," said Nikki. "And, no. You're to swim for the other side immediately. Gwen can't swim. She'll panic and try to latch onto you. She won't be able to help it. It's just an instinctive behavior with drowning victims. If she grabs you you'll both drown."

"We need something Gwen can hang onto," said Kira. "Wait a minute." She disappeared for a second and came back with her arms full of ramrods. She tied the long sticks together into a bundle using the leather strips Curio had pulled off the ropes. "These should float. Gwen can drop them into the water right before she jumps."

A loud clanging sound came from the stairs.

"I think they're trying to hammer the portcullis down," said Nikki. "We need to hurry." She handed Kira a rope. "Start pulling it apart. We need long threads."

Nikki took the length she'd knotted together and carried it to the first cannon in the row. She tied a thick knot about a foot from the end and stuffed the knot into the fuse hole of the cannon. Then she stretched the thread to the next cannon and did the same thing. She'd finished five cannons when Kira came running up to her.

"Here's some more," she said, handing Nikki a long length of thread already knotted together.

Kira ran back to the hay bale and Nikki kept linking the cannons together with the fuse. She finished the ones pointed at Cogent Town and paused at the first one in the row which pointed at Castle Cogent. She had a feeling that neither Rufius nor the Count of Calumnia would want to fire on the castle. It was the seat of power. They wanted to occupy it, not destroy it. These cannons were also close to the point on the crenellations where the coal line was attached. The last thing she wanted was for the explosion to destroy the coal line.

"Here's the last of it," said Kira, running up. "Gwen needs the rest of the ropes for Krill's harness."

"Okay," said Nikki. "I'll skip these cannons. It's the ones pointed at the town which are more important. I'll finish the fuse. You get Gwen and Curio down the stairs."

Nikki took the last of the thread and tied it to the thread on the first cannon she'd done. Then she draped the long thread along the roof and down the stairs. It only reached about halfway down. Nikki winced. She wasn't sure how quickly hemp burned. She'd have to light it and then run like hell the rest of the way down. Kira joined her on the stairs, followed by Gwen carrying Curio on her back.

"Everyone get all the way down the stairs and away from the entrance," said Nikki. "Pull Krill farther away. Pieces of shrapnel might travel all the way down." She yanked up the sleeve of her page jacket and retrieved the piece of flint and the piece of steel she'd taken from the Prince's laboratory. She waited until the others were all the way down the stairs and then with a quick motion struck the steel downward on the flint. A spark flared but failed to catch on the end of the fuse. She struck the steel again, trying to ignore the clanging coming from the portcullis down below. This time the spark caught. A thin bright line of fire raced up the stairs toward the cannons.

Nikki ran down the stairs two at a time. She was almost to the bottom when an enormous boom shook the tower. She tripped and fell head over heels. Something whizzed by her and bounced off the stone walls, sending bits of stone flying in all directions. Above her a series of even louder explosions shook the roof of the tower. She felt hands grab her and pull her away from the stairs.

"Are you all right?" asked Kira as she dragged Nikki next to Krill, who was still unconscious.

"I think so," said Nikki. "Something banged into my arm, but it's just sore, not bleeding. It must have been just a piece of stone."

"Do ya think that was all of them, Miss?" asked Curio. "All the cannons?"

"I'm not sure," said Nikki.

They sat listening. No sounds came from up on the roof, but below them the hammering had started again. Smoke was pouring down the stairs, smelling of sulfur from the gunpowder.

"We can't wait any longer," said Gwen. "They'll be through the gate soon."

Nikki nodded. "Start carrying Krill up. I'll run up and make sure there aren't any unexploded cannons."

Before the others could protest she dashed back up the stairs. The sulfurous smoke was so thick on the roof that at first she wasn't sure exactly what she was looking at. There seemed to be a large pile of stones in the middle of the roof which hadn't been there before. Then she realized that it was the remains of the guardhouse. Darius's burial mound.

She squinted through the smoke, trying to spot any remaining red sparks. To her relief she didn't see any. The cannons closest to her were smoking piles of shrapnel, their barrels split open as if by a giant can opener. She walked the entire row of cannons pointing at the town. All had been destroyed.

"Quite a good day's work," said Kira, breathing heavily from the effort of helping Gwen carry Krill. "I'd say the Prince owes us a nice roast turkey dinner, if we make it back to his mansion."

"With mashed potatoes and two pieces of cherry pie each," said Curio, hopping along on one leg.

They picked their way toward the hay bale, dodging burning-hot pieces of shrapnel scattered over the roof. There was nothing left of the hay bale but smoking cinders.

Nikki quickly checked the coal line, giving it a firm tug. It snapped back with a twang. "It feels safe enough," she said. "I'll go first. Kira, you help Gwen get Krill into the harness, then follow me. Curio, you'll have to go last. Everyone, make sure you don't jump until you're near the middle of the moat. The water's shallow near the edge. If you can, try to keep your arms by your side when you hit the water."

It was a very long drop, but Nikki felt it was pointless to say so. They all knew it. And they all knew they had no choice. She sat on the edge of the roof and grabbed the coal line with both hands. Then she hooked both legs around the line and slowly eased her weight off the edge until she was hanging in the air. Her arms immediately felt the strain. She inched forward along the upward sloping line, sweat pouring from her face after only a few feet. She felt the line rebound as Kira climbed on. At first the extra movement made the upward climb even more difficult, buy then they instinctively began to match each other's motion.

Nikki twisted her neck and looked down. Far below the moat sparkled in the moonlight. Almost there. She wrenched herself upward another few feet and stopped. "Are you ready?" she asked.

"Yes," came Kira's faint reply.

Nikki unhooked her legs and hung by her hands. Her sweaty hands gave her no choice. She was going to fall whether she wanted to or not. As she lost her hold she shut her eyes tightly, remembering at the last second to flatten her arms to her sides. She hit the water with brutal impact, going down, down, until her feet felt the muddy bottom of the moat. She pushed off and swam desperately up toward the surface.

She came up gasping just as Kira plunged into the moat a few feet away. Nikki tread water and glanced up. Gwen and Curio were both on the coal line. Gwen had a loop of rope around her shoulders and she was pulling Krill's limp body along as he hung in the harness. She could tell it was taking an immense effort. Every few feet Gwen had to rest, hanging with her head drooping, taking one arm off the line to shake it out, then the other. Curio was trying to help by pushing at Krill's feet, but it didn't seem to be doing much good.

Nikki glanced over at the still steaming hole they'd made in the wall of the laundry room. A flapping sheet partially covered it, but there didn't seem to be anyone looking out. She wondered if the Count of Calumnia had called all his guards up to the roof.

Kira surfaced next to her.

"Gwen needs to go farther," said Kira, looking up. "She's still too close to the shallows."

"I think she knows," said Nikki. "But I'm not sure if she *can* go farther. I'm amazed she's managing at all. I could barely pull *myself* up."

They watched helplessly as Gwen hung motionless from the coal line.

Curio seemed to sense that she couldn't go any farther. Far below Nikki and Kira gasped as he dropped his legs from the coal line and hung from his hands. He slowly swung himself forward, hand over hand, bumping along Krill's limp body until he reached Gwen. He snagged the rope around her shoulders with one foot and slowly, painfully, inch by inch he pulled Krill forward using his foot. His efforts seemed to rally Gwen. She started forward again and together they managed to pull Krill up another ten feet.

"Far enough!" Nikki shouted up at them. "Drop Krill! Now!" She didn't care who heard her. They needed to drop Krill into the water before they became so exhausted they fell from the coal line and left him hanging there.

Gwen pulled a knife from her sleeve and sawed at Krill's harness. She got his shoulders loose and then his knees. He fell.

Nikki and Kira swam frantically toward the place where he hit. They dived at the same time.

It was too dark too see. Nikki swam blindly down toward the bottom of the moat. Nothing. She felt her lungs straining as she swam back and forth in a grid pattern. Something hit her in the face. It was Kira's long braids. She felt Kira grab her by the shoulder and force something into her hand. It was Krill's leather tunic. Together they struggled to pull him to the surface.

"Is he breathing?" gasped Kira.

"I'm not sure," said Nikki, gulping air. "No time. Get him to the other bank."

Kira grabbed her brother around the neck with one arm and back-stroked toward the bank.

Nikki looked up just as Curio hit the water nearby. He popped up like a little cork almost immediately and began dog-paddling toward Kira and Krill.

Gwen was still on the coal line. She had dropped the bundle of ramrods which had been tied to Krill's harness, but she was hanging by her hands and seemed unable to let go.

"Gwen . . ." Nikki began. Suddenly spurts of water exploded all around her. She looked up at the top of the tower. The Count's guards had made it through the iron portcullis and were shooting arrows at her from the roof.

"Gwen!" she shouted. "Drop before . . ."

Too late. Gwen cried out, hit by an arrow. She fell.

Nikki reached her right as she hit the water. She grabbed Gwen's hair just before her head disappeared below the water and began a frantic side-stroke toward the far bank of the moat. Gwen didn't resist. Her limp body floated along, her pale cotton dress billowing around her. The arrows splashing down beside them thinned out as they gradually moved out of range.

"Here, I've got her," said Kira, swimming up and hooking her arm around Gwen's neck.

Together they dragged Gwen out of the water and up the rocky bank. Curio was waiting beside Krill on the far side of the low stone wall surrounding the moat.

Nikki and Kira laid Gwen down and collapsed against the wall.

"What now?" gasped Kira.

Nikki shook her head, too exhausted to answer.

"We can't stay here, Miss," said Curio. "Them guards may be all up on the roof, but soon enough they'll come down and spot us."

"Well then it's a good thing I happened along when I did," said a voice.

They jumped up as Fuzz appeared out of the darkness. He knelt down by Krill and then Gwen. "They're alive," he said. "But it's not good. They're both in bad shape, especially Krill. He's barely got a pulse. The arrow's in Gwen's upper back. I don't think it's near any vital organs, but she's bleeding heavily. We need to get them to Linnea and her healers as soon as possible."

"How?" said Nikki in despair. She didn't feel she had even an ounce of strength left.

"Harvey," said Fuzz. He darted back into the darkness and re-turned leading an enormous Clydesdale. "Not sure that's his given name, but it suits him. One of the Knights of the Iron Fist was riding him. It's probably better if you don't ask what happened to the Knight. Let's just say that the imps are in a vengeful mood after the invasion of ImpHaven. Come on. Everybody climb on. Harvey's big enough to carry all of us."

Between them they managed to drape Gwen and Krill across the huge horse's back. Fuzz climbed on and grabbed the reins. Curio, Nikki, and Kira sat all in a row behind him and they clip-clopped their way along the dark streets of Cogent Town toward the mansion of the Prince of Physics.

# Chapter Eleven

## Partings

"**B**UT I DON'T see why I need to be here," whined the King, sitting on his carved wooden throne in the throne room of Castle Cogent. "It's not even dawn yet and I was sound asleep. I'm sure you and Bertie can handle things between you."

A flash of contempt passed across the scarred face of the Prince of Physics. "Your Highness, you are still the ruler of the Realm. There are serious issues to be decided and they have to be decided quickly." He paced in front of the throne. "An attempt was just made to overthrow you. It nearly succeeded. If it weren't for the actions of many brave citizens the Realm would now be in the hands of murderous thugs."

"Yes, yes," said the King impatiently. "I'll hand out medals tomorrow. Right now I need thirty more winks. Have my servants wake me at noon." He rose from the throne, but the Prince gave him such a ferocious glare that he plopped back down.

The imps, farmers, fishermen, pirates, clerks, servants, pages and castle guards gathered in the throne room looked nervously from the King to the Prince.

Fuzz, Athena, and Bertie were seated on the dais just below the throne. At a nudge from Athena Bertie reluctantly stood up and faced the King.

"Uncle," began Bertie. He paused for a long time, looking up at the ceiling, apparently for inspiration. Athena stretched her un-injured leg out and kicked him.

Bertie jumped, turned red, and nearly fell off the dais. The Prince of Physics grabbed him and gave him a shake.

"Right," said Bertie. "Awfully sorry. A little bit of nerves is all." He cleared his throat. "Uncle, we've been talking." He gestured at himself, Athena, Fuzz, and the Prince. "The conclusion we've come to is that I should take over your duties. Become King, to put it flatly. Not really a job I ever coveted, to be honest. But others here think it's a good idea. And there's a lot of benefit in the idea. For you, I mean. Just think of all the free time you'll have. You can play lawn tennis every day. Sleep as long as you like. Take that trip to the southern beaches you've been putting off. Now, many here would say that I have no experience with ruling the Realm. And they'd be right. But someone's got to do it, and I am the next in line for the throne. And of course I'd have plenty of help. The Prince here has promised to stay in Cogent Town until I've got things under control. And your loyal emissaries will be by my side every day."

Fuzz winced when he heard the words "every day", but he stood up and took a bow.

Athena was still unable to stand on her injured leg, but she waved as regally as any queen.

"So," continued Bertie, "what do you say, Uncle? I know you've been tired of the job for a long while now. We aren't insisting, of course. If you want to stay King I'm sure everyone here will be happy to obey your orders. You'll need to start issuing orders right and left, of course. There's no end of work to be done at the moment. Cogent Town is in a miserable state of affairs after the battle. Houses all over town are still burning. Many citizens have been killed or injured. We're still hunting down the last remaining Knights of the Iron Fist. Down south, ImpHaven is in ruins and will need manpower and supplies from the Realm to help rebuild. And up here in the north someone tried to destroy Clearwater dam. The brave pirates from Kingston stopped the plot in time, but one side of the dam was damaged and needs immediate repairs."

At the back of the throne room Nikki was listening to the proceedings while petting Cation. Cation had wandered from the Prince's mansion back up castle hill on her own and had again taken up her role as chief mouser of Castle Cogent. Nikki stood on her tip toes to get a look at the King's face. He looked horrified. She strongly suspected that his horror was not due to the damage suffered by the town and its citizens, but due to the mountains of work needed to set things right again.

"He looks like a fat infant who's just had his bottle taken away," whispered Curio, who was standing next to Nikki. "Now, maybe a pedestal baby like myself shouldn't say such things about a King, but I don't knows as I care. Peoples has died. Like Mr. Darius. Now, I knows he wasn't no friend to the imps and that did him no credit, but it was very brave of him to take on the Count of Calumnia's guards. He was trying to save lives, and he died because of his bravery."

"Yes," said Nikki. "He was very brave." She knew they would never have been able to destroy the Count's cannons if Darius had not been brave enough to fight the Count's guards and bring down the portcullis. Thinking of him made her think of Gwen. Gwen had been deeply in love with him. The look on her face as she cradled his dead body on top of the tower had proved that. But Darius's hatred of the imps had been painful to Gwen. Nikki thought it would take Gwen a long time to reconcile the love and the hatred. Fortunately she wouldn't have to grapple with it right away. Linnea the Healer had given her something to induce sleep after removing the arrow from her back. Gwen was recovering in a guest room at the mansion of the Prince of Physics. As was Krill. Krill had barely survived, having lost a severe amount of blood. After cleaning his wound

Linnea had drawn blood from Kira and transfused it into Krill. Nikki had been horrified when she'd learned about it. The Realm of Reason was not nearly advanced enough to know about blood types. Linnea had simply gotten lucky that Kira and Krill happened to have the same blood type. Either that or Krill just happened to have blood type AB Positive. People with AB Positive were universal recipients. They could safely receive any blood type during a transfusion. People with other blood types would die if given the wrong type. Nikki had thought about trying to explain blood types to Linnea to prevent her killing someone in the future, but she'd abandoned the idea. The Realm didn't have the medical technology necessary to do ABO typing of red blood cells. So she had no evidence to show the healer what she was talking about. She'd just have to hope that Linnea didn't try blood transfusions on a regular basis.

"Well, your Highness?" asked the Prince of Physics, none too politely. "What will it be? Abdication? Or will you continue on the throne? If so I will need to consult with you immediately. We need to distribute coin from your treasury to help the people of Cogent Town rebuild. And we need to send stonemasons up to Clearwater dam to start repairs as soon as possible so that more of the dam doesn't collapse. It is already leaking too much water. The Clearwater River is overflowing its banks and homes along the river are flooding."

The King shook his head mutely. "I . . ." he began, then stopped and stared at the floor.

Nikki felt a bit sorry for him. He wasn't a bad person, really. He was just in over his head. He'd never been cut out for the job of King. She didn't know much about monarchies, but from what she'd observed the role of King in the Realm of Reason was not just a ceremonial job. The King had to do actual work and make day to day decisions, kind of like the mayor of a large city. He had to ensure that the economy ran smoothly, that enough food was grown for everyone, that the streets were kept clean, and that crime wasn't allowed to flourish. It was a big job and the King wasn't up to it. For that matter, Bertie wasn't really up to it either. Nikki strongly suspected that Bertie had been forced to volunteer for the role by Athena.

Nikki was jolted out of her thoughts when Curio suddenly bumped against her.

"Sorry, Miss," whispered Curio. "I'm not steady on me feet yet. I keeps listing to one side like a boat in a storm."

"It's okay," said Nikki, giving him her arm to lean on. Curio had lost two outer toes on his right foot, from the coal line cutting into it on his slide down to the tower. Linnea had sewed up the wound and given him a cane to lean on, but it had to be very painful. Curio never complained, and had refused various offers to be carried around on the backs of Griff's surviving crew members.

There was a commotion up at the dais. Nikki stood on her tip toes again.

Athena had risen from her chair. Fuzz jumped up to help her. She leaned on his arm and faced the King.

"Your Highness," said Athena in a voice of steel, "you will abdicate the throne this instant. There is much to be done and you are not up to the task. There is no more to be said. Lives will be lost if we delay. Your nephew will take the throne, and Fuzz, myself, and the Prince will help him in his duties with all the strength we have."

Athena sat back down.

The King stared at the back of her head in an astonished but also relieved sort of way. He nodded slowly and removed his crown. He rose from the throne and handed the crown to Bertie.

Bertie took it as if it was red-hot and burning his hands, but at a curt nod from the Prince he put it on his head.

The King descended from the dais and walked slowly through the crowd in the throne room. Some of the crowd wept, but most looked relieved. Two guards opened the throne room doors for the King and he was gone.

Nikki never did find out what happened to him. Her best guess was that he retired to long lazy days of playing lawn tennis and taking naps.

Over the next few weeks Nikki helped out where she could, delivering food and blankets to the townspeople whose homes had been destroyed, carrying buckets of water to put out the smoldering remains of the fires caused by Geber's fireworks. At night she slept in a small tower room in Castle Cogent, not far from Curio's room. Curio had been made a King's Emissary by Bertie. Because of his injury Curio was not able to perform his errands on foot as was customary for an emissary, so Bertie had given him a donkey from the castle stables. Curio had named her Daisy and he rode her proudly up and down the streets of Cogent Town, delivering food to hungry citizens and taking messages from Bertie to the nobles in town who had proved their loyalty to the Realm.

No one knew what had happened to Rufius. Many of the Knights of the Iron Fist had been killed. The remainder had been captured and thrown in the dungeons of Castle Cogent. Geber's dead body had been found, and the Mystic men had disappeared back into their mountain hideout. But Rufius, who had been the trigger for all the destruction, was nowhere to be found.

Bertie and Fuzz sent out Rounders to search for him. Most of the Rounders had not participated in the battle of Cogent Town, and Fuzz had decided that giving them a second chance was the best option. The castle guards had also stayed out of the fighting. Many of the citizens who'd lost loved ones thought that the guards should stand trial for this. But Bertie and the Prince of Physics argued that it was the guards' sworn duty to follow orders from the King, and that the King had not given them any orders. Nikki thought this was a bit of a weak argument, and that the castle guards should have helped out their fellow citizens, but it wasn't up to her.

The Lurkers were not so lucky. Bertie ordered all of them to leave the Realm and never return. Nikki had her doubts about how many of them actually did so. She suspected that some of them used their talents for subterfuge and sneakiness to change their appearance and hide among the citizenry.

When Gwen had recovered from her arrow wound Bertie went to the Prince's mansion to visit her and offered her the post that Geber had held. The King's Alchemist. Gwen had accepted and had immediately started on her first task, overseeing the strengthening and repairing of Clearwater dam.

Once Krill had recovered he and Kira started on the journey back to their ship, which was anchored at Kingston. Griff and her surviving crew travelled with them and welcomed them back to a life of cod fishing and the occasional bit of pirating now and then.

One evening Athena and Fuzz came to visit Nikki in her room at the castle.

"I have a present for you, Miss," said Athena, leaning heavily on Fuzz's arm. "I would like to give it to you now, before you leave."

"Leave?" asked Nikki in surprise.

"Yes, Miss," said Athena with a sad smile. "To go home. It is time. I know you miss your mother and your home. We knew from the start that you would not stay here in the Realm forever."

The imp handed Nikki a scroll tied with a red satin ribbon.

Nikki unrolled it. "Oh," she said with a laugh. "It's all my favorite logical fallacies. Appeal to popularity, appeal to authority, ad hominem, false dilemma, straw man, counting the hits, and post hoc."

"Yes, Miss," said Athena. "I had the castle scribe copy them from my parchments. I wanted a souvenir of our time together. I have a copy and I also gave a copy to little Curio and to Miss Gwendolyn."

Nikki bent down and gave the imp a hug. "Thanks Athena. I don't know what to say. I've been so busy that I haven't really thought about leaving. I guess I knew I would eventually, but it's been one thing after another here in the Realm. There hasn't really been any time to be homesick." She scooped up Cation, who was curling herself around her ankles.

"Your kitten has grown up, Miss," said Athena. "I have heard from the servants here in the castle that she is quite the mouser. If you decide to leave her here she will be well taken care of."

Nikki looked down at the cat purring in her arms and tears filled her eyes. "I know she belongs here in the Realm," she said, her voice breaking, "but do you think I could possibly take her with me?"

Athena looked concerned. "I am not sure, Miss. I do not know if we have ever had an animal pass through the Cogent Town portal before."

"There was that blasted sheep," said Fuzz. "Remember? It was years ago. I went through the portal, just to make sure it was still functioning. And a sheep followed me in. We landed in some meadow I'd never seen before and the stupid animal took off at a run. Took me forever to catch it and shove it back through the portal to the Realm. Anyway, it was fine. No harm came to it. Me, on the other hand, I had a sore arm for days afterward from all the sheep wrestling."

Nikki nodded. "Then I think I'd like to take Cation with me. It sounds like she'll be okay."

"As you wish, Miss," said Athena. "We will call for you tomorrow morning."

"Tomorrow?" asked Nikki, feeling a sudden wave of panic. "I'm going through the portal tomorrow?"

"We think it best, Miss," said Athena. "You've been in the Realm a long time. Nearly a year by our reckoning. No time will have passed in your realm, of course. Do not worry on that score. Your mother will not have even noticed your absence. But we think it best for you to return. If you stay much longer you may begin to feel divided loyalties to the two realms. That could be painful for you. It will be better if you return to your old life."

Nikki wiped away a tear. "Will I remember you? And Curio? And

Gwen? And the Realm of Reason?"

Athena patted her arm. "Of course, Miss. The portal does not wipe your memory. You will remember everything that has happened here. And you will retain fond memories of the friends you have made here. And we will remember you as well."

"Come on old girl," said Fuzz, pulling Athena toward the door as Nikki started to cry. "Let's leave her in peace." He turned at the door and looked back at Nikki. "Don't worry," he said. "I'll round up everyone and we'll all give you a big send off. You'll have plenty of time to say your good byes."

NIKKI TUGGED AT the woolen trousers Fuzz had found for her. They were too long, but at a pinch they could pass for something that people in her world wore. She had replaced her velvet page jacket with her Westlake Debate Team t-shirt. Her Nikes had long since disintegrated, so her feet were bare. She tried to smile bravely at the small group of people gathered in the alleyway leading to the portal, but she could tell that her smile was more of a grimace of pain. She was going to miss them all horribly. Curio, Gwen, Athena, Fuzz. She gave them all a long hug. Kira, Krill, Linnea, Griff and the Prince of Physics she had already said good bye to. They had left to return to their homes in Kingston.

Curio pulled a bouquet of yellow roses from Daisy the Donkey's saddle bag. He wiped a grubby hand across his eyes and held out the roses. "Here ya go, Miss," he said with a sniffle. "I hope these'll do. I didn't know yer favorite color."

Nikki hugged him again. "They're lovely. I hope I can come back here someday, Curio. I'm sure in a few years you'll already be a top advisor to the King."

"Don't know about that, Miss," said Curio. "But I'll do me best." He petted Cation, who was wrapped around Nikki's neck. "Good bye,

Miss." He turned abruptly away.

Gwen stepped forward and handed Nikki a silver bracelet. "It's not as good as a real jeweler could do," she said, "but I smelted the silver myself. It's from the mines in the Haunted Hills."

Nikki tucked Curio's roses under her arm and put the bracelet on. "Thanks Gwen," she said with a catch in her throat. "You'll remember what I said, won't you? About the black powder?"

Gwen frowned slightly, but she nodded. "Yes, of course. Though I still think you're underestimating how much good it could do. Especially in mining and tunnel-building. But I'll keep your warning of its dangers in mind."

Nikki nodded. It was the best she could do. It was up to Gwen now, and the rest of the Realm, whether or not they continued along a path that led to guns and all their horrors. She adjusted Cation on her neck and checked that she still had Curio's roses and Athena's scroll under her arm. "I guess I'm ready," she said.

Athena and Fuzz walked beside her to the portal entrance. It was just a fuzzy, gray, door-shaped hole in the wall of the alley.

Nikki froze. She had a sudden vision of herself spinning wildly in outer space, unable to return home or return to the Realm.

Athena patted her arm. "It is all right, Miss. The portal is perfectly safe. We do not understand its workings, but we have never been lost inside it, unable to return home. It has always sent us safely back to the Realm."

Nikki nodded. "I . . ."

"It is best to go quickly, Miss," said Athena, giving her a gentle push.

Nikki took a deep breath and stepped through.

The twirling and spinning in space that she'd been imagining didn't happen. One second she was standing in the alleyway next to Fuzz and Athena, the next second she was climbing out of the rusty old boiler at the back of the janitor's closet at her high school. The smell of ammonia and floor wax tickled her nose. Cation was purring contentedly in her ear.

Nikki climbed over stacks of old newspapers and piles of buckets and oily cleaning rags. It was dark, and the closet seemed bigger than she remembered it. A small noise came from somewhere near the door to the hallway. She froze, wondering if the rats which occasionally wandered into the school cafeteria had made a nest in the closet. As she cautiously approached the door she realized that the noise had been made by something much bigger than a rat. A man was at the door, his back to her. He turned the door handle and a sliver of light shone on his wavy black hair. His long black tunic and leather sandals were illuminated for an instant, and then he was gone.

Nikki sank down onto a pile of newspapers.

Rufius was in her high school.

# End of Book Eight

Nikki's adventures in the Realm of Reason have come to an end.

### The Logic to the Rescue series
*Logic to the Rescue*
*The Prince of Physics*
*The Bard of Biology*
*Mystics and Medicine*
*The Sorcerer of the Stars*
*Warlock of the Wind*
*The Engineer of Evil*
*Math and Manners*

### The Hamsters Rule series
*Hamsters Rule, Gerbils Drool*
*Hamsters Rule the School*

Made in the USA
Las Vegas, NV
05 July 2022

51123779R10094